CW00872040

Through The Gate

An Avalon Myst Novel

S. L. Seib

Through The Gate: An Avalon Myst Novel, is a work of fiction. All incidents and dialogue, and all characters are products of the authors imagination and are not to be considered as real. Any resemblance to persons living or dead is entirely coincidental.

Copyright @ 2017

All Rights Reserved.

Published in Canada by
S.L.Seib

www.slseib.com

First Edition

*To my loving family and friends for all their support
and encouragement.
You're The Best!*

Chapter One

A pair of big brown eyes framed in strong cheekbones stared into the red, beat up Voltswagen rearview mirror. Aurora looked at her mother's reflection and that of her own in distain. It was just the two of them ever since she could remember. Her mother held her gaze, silently pleading for the slightest bit of understanding. Aurora didn't get why they had to move; giving up everything they had worked so hard to obtain, just to start over in an unfamiliar and uncomfortable place.

The old family estate came into view as the car turned the last winding corner. For hours now the two had endured the tediously long trip down roads that led to unmarked forks, roads of which were lined with the all too familiar forests of Northern Labrador. If it weren't for Emily's acute sense of direction, they would have been lost in the middle of nowhere ages ago.

The car slowed to a cautious crawl as the sight of a once beautiful country estate stood weakly in disrepair. The gate stood ajar: rusted, bent and broken and the cobblestone wall it was attached to was overgrown with a heavy layer of moss and vines. The grass rose up passed the car's grill, being impatiently mowed over by the old beast of a machine. Emily stuck her head out the window just to judge where they were going. Oddly shaped trees and bushes grew within the massive yard, all grey and leafless, making the grounds seem like a haunted graveyard. Various weathered statues were strewn with the random assortments of the now very wild foliage. There was every different colour that can be grown naturally within that stone wall, yet both girls knew there wasn't a specific design to any of it.

The car lurched to a halt, wheels spinning wildly in the deep pile of mud amidst the mini swamp of grass. Aurora simply stared at what lay before her, her mind trying to make sense of the information her eyes took in. Her face went blank with her mouth slightly agape, Emily purposely avoiding her daughter's vacant expression.

"This can't seriously be it..." The daughter muttered in disbelief.

Emily frowned as the car pulled itself from the pit of muddy hell. She sighed heavily as she pulled up as close to the house as she could. "... What's wrong with it? It's very spacious and close to town..."

"Mom, please. This place is a complete disaster!" She exclaimed with as much abhorrence she could muster. "I mean look at it... Broken and falling to pieces, Mom? I don't think there's not a rotten piece of wood in the lot! It should be condemned, not lived in..." Aurora jumped out of the car as it puttered there, stranded in another petite sea of mud. It was an Elizabethan styled manor at one point, but the serious lack of care left it ugly and in serious need of some TLC.

The once elegant milling work upon the outside veranda had long been rotten and in need of replacing. The Shutters had fallen off their hinges to feed the mass of plants beneath as fertilizer. The only window at the front that was not cracked or completely shattered was the one in the attic, a beautiful stain glass masterpiece crafted in the shape of a lotus flower. Everything about the house, even the land surrounding it, seemed as though it had not been touched for eons. Aurora could tell the house had been a beautiful glowing white once upon a time, but all that was left were chips here and there upon the ground; a vague indication that this house used to be the pride of the surrounding area.

"Wait, Aurora help me unpack first!" her mother called after her as Aurora continued her unpleasant venture across the overgrown lawn, making sure to acknowledge every flaw so as to complain about it later to a mother who refused to be moved.

There were three steps leading up to the veranda, two of which were cracked, whether-beaten and torn off their track. Aurora lept over them and landed shakily upon the uneven floor, trying hard not to fall through the floor boards. Tip-toeing across the way with every single board squealing a different note, Aurora turned the surprisingly shiny handle to the front door. A loud screech echoed through the quiet morning air as the last hinge that hung to the frame cried out in protest and pulled itself from the wood, toppling to the ground as Aurora stood there in shock. "You've got to be shittin' me..." She mumbled under her breath, staring at the newly painted door at her feet. "The whole place is a death trap..."

Her mother gleefully strolled to the entrance, half of her belongings piled high in her arms, glancing at the door lying dully on the ground. "What'd you do that for?!" She exclaimed, oblivious to the sny look her daughter was giving her. Aurora rolled her eyes dramatically and strode inside, grabbing one of her bags from her mother and draping it over the shoulder.

The inside wasn't much different, nothing but the smell of old dirt, mould and animal urine. Everything was covered in old sheets and plastic, all of which were covered in a fine layer of dust. Aurora's nose began twitching diligently as sneeze after sneeze escaped her grasp.

Emily clumsily dropped the boxes by the staircase and whipped out something out of her back pocket. Handing Aurora a cloth mask, Emily calmly walked over to the nearest window. She pulled the large sheet of plastic off of the grimy pane and quickly opening the window just in time for a gust of wind to blow the dust all over Aurora's annoyed grimace. Once again Aurora sneezed, coughed and nearly gagged as she hurried to put the mask over her face. Emily did that for every window on the main floor, each time forcing more dust and god knows what else into Aurora's disgruntled face.

She turned to Aurora, noticing she hadn't moved an inch and had a wide eyed look-to-kill expression on her face, "Why don't you find yourself a room upstairs and set yourself up, Hun?". Emily said cheerfully, handing her daughter a large dufflebag. Aurora growled and began climbing the intensely creaky and dusty stairs, mumbling strings of profanities along the way.

For a brief moment, Aurora saw a little fuzz-ball scurry across the steps "Note to self: We have rats..." She mumbled solemnly as she began popping her head into each grotesquely rodent-infested room, including the bathroom which she was sure would need to be sterilized by burning.

Finally she chose one that needed the least bit of cleaning and plunked her things sloppily upon the floor. There was a lot that needed to be cleaned yet and Aurora didn't want to even think about how much of a headache it would equal up to in the end. A new school, new friends, new life... Change in any form is hard to accept, and greatly uncalled for.

Aurora opened the bedroom curtains and for a second, was pleased with the elegant beauty the room had to offer. Her foot slipped in some goop and she nearly toppled to the floor where more goop awaited. It wasn't just rats they had, their winged cousins seemed to make a home there as well.

"Mum, why do we have to live *here*?" She yelled over the stair's railings, trying hard not to touch anything. "Wouldn't it have been easier to just get like a two bedroom house or apartment or something? Like *come on*, this place reeks!-"

"Aurora just give it a chance... It may need work now, but it will be quite the home in a couple months!" Her mother pleaded as she climbed the noisy stairs. "And besides, it's not like we had much choice-"

"Mother please..."

"You know the only way to deal with our debts was to sell the house, and besides... now we get a real piece of history all to ourselves!" She exclaimed quietly. Aurora knew what her mother was thinking but didn't have the guts to say.

"... Mum... how are we going to pay to repair this...?" Her mother looked her square in the eyes, suddenly seeing as much fear in her daughters gaze as there was in her own. The woman swallowed hard and tried ever so desperately to put on her fake-motherly-smile. She gently took Aurora's hand in hers and compared the two: A young, vibrant, silky smooth hand encrusted in gaudy rings and bright blue nail polish compared to the plain, wrinkled, rough, hard hands of an aged woman... to the naked eye they would be completely different in every way. To her, all she saw was her daughter trying to be something she wasn't. She missed the times when she could talk to her about everything and anything; she missed her sweet, doting Aurora.

"... I'll have to work two jobs then... It'll all work out, I promise. Now go have yourself a little adventure." She smiled, remembering Aurora as a tyke running around the town in a pirate suit. Aurora gruffly muttered some undesirable words and ran down the stairs.

"Children have adventures Mum, I'm too old to do any of that stupid ass bull shit..." Aurora ran out the front, anger pumping through her veins. She wasn't a child anymore. 15 is much more than an acceptable age for being married with kids and what-not in other countries, so how could she still be considered a kid! At least, that's what ran through her mind before she stubbed her toes on a stone that jutted out from the path and began swearing every curse that had ever crossed her lips. Her anger slowly subsided with the pain as she gazed around accusingly, ready to bite the head off the first living thing that showed its face. Naturally, there was nothing, so she instead turned her attention to the path she had stumbled upon.

The slate stone pathway wound all the way around the building, as did the consistent colour gradient of brown and grey plants that marked the signs of careless gardening. Amidst all the dead foliage and trellises for vines was a magnificent marbled fountain placed elegantly in the middle. It seemed so out of place with its gleaming surface cascading ripples of light off of other variously placed items, an angel stood perched upon the mountainous lode with its arms outstretched as though it were presenting something grand and heavenly. Its eyes glowed blue in the sun and under closer inspection, Aurora discovered that the eyes were large sapphire jewels, gazing at her in a hopeful acknowledgement of forgotten truth. She gazed over it as though she were an artist critique and was baffled at it's great detail and it's odd presence amidst a place so full of decay and death.

Staring past the fountain, Aurora caught sight of something rather unusual in the corner of the garden. Sitting snugly between conjoining cobblestone walls stood a shining silvery arch, covered in different vines and flowers, the likes of which seemed foreign and beautiful. A small chill ran down her spine and a sense of deja-vu radiated through her consciousness. There was something very familiar about that gateway that was tantalizingly invigorating. Before Aurora knew it, her feet had led her through it and onto the path that lay beyond.

Her curiosity knew no bounds as she slowly strolled down the various ingrown paths, to what end she wasn't sure. What was minutes felt like hours as she made her way through the maze of trees. Deeper and deeper into the established, yet unknown, grove she crept, curiosity turning more into an odd sense of uncomfortable caution. She stopped, looked back down the path and realized she hadn't even wandered far from the house yet. A small chuckle erupted from her lips as she realized that she did exactly what her Mother advised to do... "-Adventure..." She mumbled, shaking her head from the irony. She also noticed off to her left, a little cote, barely discernible from the surrounding brush, "Right on..."

The cote was old but in much better shape than the manor, almost like a home-away-from-mansion. It reminded her of an olden day greenhouse, with a glass ceiling reinforced with weathered copper bars and intricately carved windows upon the aged grey walls. Cautiously entering through the elegantly stained glass door, her eyes immediately fell to the table and chair in the right hand corner. Little saplings sprouted out of the cracks in the floorboards and lit up the little building with their gentle green youth. The cote seemed quaint yet elegant with it's calm blue walls and stained white floors. Old faded pictures were placed on the wall of people Aurora couldn't immediately place. The whole place was charming in every sense of the word.

On the table sat an old hurricane lantern and a marvellously engraved wooden box. Aurora quickly sat next to the table and opened the mystery box, curiosity percolating inside her jittery belly. It was a book.

Aurora glanced at it quizzically, picking it up and inspecting the cover, which was so worn; it no longer had the title etchings on it. Opening it to the first page, an instant smile was plastered all over her face. Jane Austen's 'Pride and Prejudice', Aurora's favorite read. An old picture fell out of the pages and onto the dirt floor. Picking it up, Aurora saw that it viewed an uncanny resemblance to her... very uncanny; almost identical. Shocked and a bit confused she flipped the picture over and read what was written. *'Emilia Clanilla 3'*. It was her grandmother.

She thumbed through the pages of the book and noticed a bit of scribbling on one of the blank pages. It was very sloppily written, faded and made no sense in the slightest. *'It will wrap around the arch and crawl down the spine, bring you back to where secrets tell lies.'* Aurora raised her brows, going over the words in her head a couple more times and put the book back into the box. Shoving the picture into her pocket she rushed out the door, eager to show her mother the chilling picture of her Grandma.

Excitement ran through her as she jogged down the now beaten path to the house. It took mere minutes to get back to the unfortunately familiar withered manor, a lot shorter than finding her new little hidey-hole that might prove to make her new life more bearable. She ran by the kitchen window, which was wide open, letting all the boxed up musty smell out of the house. Her mother sat at the table, head in her hand and tears running down her cheeks. An old oval frame was clutched tightly with her white and shaky fingers. Aurora watched on in confusion; part of her wanted to rush in and give her mother an enormous bear-hug to make her feel better, and the other part was frozen in place, afraid to show that emotion she hated to expel. Between mumbled sobs and discernible sentences, Aurora made out little blitz of words. Finally, her words began to mould properly out into the open, words Aurora had never believed would come from her mother's lips.

"Oh Ma... You were right. You were so very right about him- about Aurora and everything you had predicted, Ma... I can't handle her anymore, I can't- can't..." A loud sobbing sigh escaped through the silence. "The lies I've had to tell her... the secrets and lies, Ma. I can't tell her-but I have to. I can't smile for her anymore- she's tearing me apart from the inside out... I hate her so much-what she's become... I hate being the mother..." A new wave of tears cascaded down her face as she cupped it in her hands. "I hate lying to protect you."

Aurora stood there paralyzed, mind racing with what it could all mean. Secrets? Lies? Protecting her? Aurora's hand reached up to her face and she realized that she too was crying. Did she know it all along somehow, deep down in her subconscious? *'She hates being my Mum...'*

A numbing chill began to cloud her perspiring thoughts as she realized that she had stumbled across something she never should have known. With massive fear and panic she fled into the trees. She shouldn't have been there watching her, she shouldn't even be there at the homestead at all! Whatever secrets that her mother hid from her, they were definitely big... massive, gaping, and dangerous to her right now. Change was one thing, but learning your whole life may have been a lie, nearly broke her mind.

Aurora stopped suddenly, shaking the frustrating panicky feeling clinging to her thoughts and began to cling to the only thing that would keep her semi-sane, maybe it isn't as bad as all that. Maybe it is something small. Maybe she was adopted or born with a tail or something- something that isn't a complete life-ending-deal-breaker. Taking a deep breath she looked at the wild that now surrounded her. The sun glistened just above the canopy, as if winking its little secrets into her nerve-wrecked face, meaning it would soon become dark. Evening birds called out through the woods as a slight breeze happily whispered through the forest. As beautiful as everything was, it soon came to a realization, that she had become entangled within the vastness of forest that encased the little manor. She was lost.

Aurora wound through the trees, trying desperately to remember what paths she had taken just moments ago. Shadows lurked behind every tree and the whispers of nature's children greeted her acutely hypersensitive ears. Tears gently began to rain down her face as she took one more turn around the fork. Now more than anything she wanted her mother to come grab her hand and guide her back home.

Stumbling out of the forest line and into the blinding light of the setting sun, she trotted to a stop, finding herself in the midst of something she had never before laid eyes on. Ocean water caressed the fine white sand as the great orange disc of a sun hovered above the waves. Seagulls and pelicans danced above the waves, swooping down into the ocean to catch supper for them and their families, the fish trying to escape them by jumping up into the air and being caught mid flight by yet another bird. She had never been to the ocean before. Lakes, yes, but the ocean was always a vast, far-away place that remained out of reach. What seemed even more astonishing and definitely out of place were two strange pillars of stone standing firmly upon the beach. Standing between the two, the weather carved stones opened the way to a solid walk of sand, leading out to an island a half-mile off shore. With the nagging feeling of fear now gone, she strolled along the sandbar as though she had gone down the path hundreds of times before. Had she been here when she was younger? The burdening feeling of deja-vu ate away at her stomach as the eerie sounds of the little island steadily began to meet her ears.

The island path was paved with withered sandstone and bordered with smooth, fist-sized, black stones. The birds sang more diligently than before and everything seemed to be wilder; more alive. Elegant ferns and wild flowers stretched themselves out in every direction, hoping for the sun's rays to lick their gossamer petals and leaves. Chipmunks and squirrels played amidst themselves and seemed to argue and yell at one another about which the nuts belonged to.

Everything about that magical place lifted her spirit and pulled at her memory.

The walkway ended, on the edge of a small meadow clearing to which housed a chillingly magnificent figure; ancient and awe inspiring. It was a terribly worn, blue-stoned statue of a woman holding out her hands in an offering to whoever walked that path. Her hair draped around her body, like the waves of emotion the statue imbued upon those in its presence. Fabric like water clung to the figure and made the entire statue seem to come to life. Slowly she crept towards it in awe and noticed the head-sized, oval orb upon the ground at the maiden's feet. Aurora picked it up with little effort and examined the odd symbols engraved upon its course, white surface. Tracing her fingers along the grooves, she could feel her flesh tingle with electricity. *'What on earth did I stumble upon now?'*

The rhythm of the forest began to change, forming a forceful ancient abstraction. Aurora dropped the orb as a thick caressing mist began to wrap itself around her feet. The cadence intensified as the same feeling of giddiness, fear and now anticipation melted through her with a warm, yet chilling sensation rippling down her spine. Her head began to spin as archaic tribal chants filled her mind. She closed her eyes and fell victim to the soft, moss covered earth beneath her feet.

Chapter

Two

With her head pounding, Aurora rose from her mysterious collapse and sleepily listened for the sounds of her mother making breakfast. A bird chirped loudly in her ear instead.

She bolted upright, only to lay right back down again. The sun shone cheerfully as the morning birds tweeted their melodies and rodents chattered among the trees. Dizzy and disoriented, she recalled her surroundings, remembering where she had landed herself the night before. The clearing was serene, glimmering with dragonflies and the sun's sweet rays. Confusion tugged at her brow as she realized the odd statue was replaced by a large boulder with the same kinds of markings the orb had the night before. What made her pass out so ferociously? Some new flower or maybe mould? Aurora shrugged, got back up and strolled down the walk she had come the evening before. Strange that she slept through the entire night without so much as a twitch.

Aurora reached the sand bridge where the two bodies of land met and was taken aback by the beauty of the morning's golden sunrise. Slowly she trekked down the sandbar, watching little minnows swim up to the edges and back out again. Geese paddled across the calm waters, their little ducklings following close behind. She realized how out of tune with nature she so recently had become. Her mother always loved to take walks in the northern forest hiking trails, dragging Aurora along with her for weekend trips, but not long after that, Aurora would drag her Mum to the National parks and campgrounds to get away from all the traffic and people. *'When did that change?'*

The landscape was almost as beautiful as the evening prior, only it shone a whole new life upon the wilds. A smile crossed her lips as she glanced at the morning horizon in front of her, shining so happily and readily for those that cared to see. Her eyes caught sight of the pillars and her smile began to fade. Instead of two worn and crumbled stones before her, a wondrously sculpted arch stood at length before her gaze. Aurora bit her lip in confusion... was she still dreaming?

She strode down the beach and glanced down the winding trail of forks and turns she had taken there. The path was lined with the same fist sized stones leading back to the estate. *'Is this what was there a century before? Ideas for the future? If this is a dream, it's surely an odd one to decipher...'*

The house came into view as she rounded the last turn. The silver arch glistened much more noticeably within the bright green foliage, making the fountain much more beautiful than she had left it. Aurora blinked in disbelief as she gazed upon the styling of an intact mansion. The trails that went through the garden were chalked full of healthy thriving plants; The cobblestone wall was clean and whole, with German ivy clawing its way up every stone; Windows were unbroken, stained and spotless; and the fountain, oh that beautiful fountain, was sparkling and spouting water like it never had before.

Amidst all the wonderment and beauty, crouched a boy hiding in the shadows with a terrified expression on his face. His hair was a messy tangle of curly blonde locks, and his cloths were raggedy and dirty. His face showed the same innocent youth that Aurora held, yet his stance depicted more experienced and skill than his age should allow. She stood at the arch, gaping at this new development. Should she move closer to the boy? Should she say something?

"... Hello?" Aurora called softly. His head quickly snapped to her direction, eyes wide with fright. Staring at her breathlessly, his bright eyed gaze turned from frightened to confused, cautiously glaring at her as if she would pull out a blade and slice his gullet. "What are you doing here?" She muttered harshly, not liking how he so rudely stared at her. He continued to quizzically ascertain whether she was truly a threat or not. Vile booming voices slithered to their ears as an impatient rustling sound startled both out of their stupor.

Without warning, the boy grabbed Aurora's hand and darted down the trail Aurora had just come, half dragging her at his side. Neither looked back as they wound their way through the endless trails and brush, cutting across the woods and back onto a random animal trail. The hair on the back of Aurora's neck stood on end as the grating voices were impossibly gaining pace.

Aurora glanced over her shoulder and her eyes nearly popped out of her skull at the sight of their pursuers. "Holy mother of god-what-the-hell-are-those-things!" She blurted loudly as the boy tugged at her hand.

Five grizzly monsters came barrelling after them with looks to kill on their scarred and appalling faces. The bodies were delusively buff with great blobs of fat hanging within their greasy bluish skin. They sneered and growled at their prey through rotten jagged razor-pointed teeth; their beady red eyes trying to keep them in their sights, with their long flat pig-like noses snorting and squealing alien noises as they ran... And if their appearance wasn't scary enough, the scent that fell upon the wind and into the nostrils of which ever animal that was unfortunate enough to be in its path wreaked the hideous aroma of rotting flesh, animal intestines, vomit and blood.

The chase was on, and Aurora didn't have to be dragged to want to get away from whatever those things were. She bolted ahead of the boy, yelling profanities and little yelps along the way.

The forest tilted downhill and began to thicken, dropping short into a swiftly flowing brook about a half mile down. Without warning, the boy yanked Aurora beneath a small incision in the river bank, disappearing amidst the tangled roots of a half dying tree.

The creatures stampeded to the bank and impatiently scanned the waters for floating bodies. Aurora nearly passed out trying to control her breathing and almost tossed her cookies as she caught their stench on the breeze. The two covered each others mouths as one of the creatures got far too close for comfort, sniffing and glaring into open space.

"Bleddy litta mould and peuk blikkens.... Haevin' uz flitten abouh..." One complained aloud as the creatures grudgingly made their way back up the sloped woods, pushing down trees and kicking up old logs out of frustration.

The two looked at each other, astounded that both had actually escaped the ultimate creatures of nightmares. Both released their hand from the stranger's face and looked at one another with wide eyes. Aurora wanted to laugh, but feared she still might puke if she took a deep breath.

"... I'm Peregrith..." The boy mumbled, still in the midst of aftershock.

She gazed into the quiet green eyes that exposed his innocent soul. "... A-Aurora..." She whispered back. He nodded and sat there, knees up to his chin and quietly stared at Aurora. She grinned nervously, slowly inching away. "... What?"

He just shook his head and smiled. "You.... are Aurora..." he muttered, a puzzled look of disbelief fermenting on his face. "Why have you come back?"

Her brows knit together in frustrated confusion. "...I've never been here before."

His smile broadened as realization suddenly hit him square in the face, "... I see." He muttered plainly with a smirk, knowing that he knew something that for some great reason, she did not.

Aurora curled up like the boy, resting her chin on her knees, and closed her eyes. More and more this little *Adventure* she was having, felt like the beginning of *Alice in Wonderland*. She didn't recall eating any mushrooms or anything recently though, and this dream-like state felt a lot more real than any nightmare ever was. *'I must be in a coma...'* She concluded.

Peregrith rose still smirking, and offered his hand to her. "Well Milady, it seems as though you need a guide." Aurora glanced up at his hand, still unsure if she should even trust the guy.

With a whole-hearted sigh, she sloughed off the gesture and jumped to her feet. The boy shrugged it off and tilted his head towards the rough path leading further into the woods. "Shall we?..."

Chapter
Three

The main path ran parallel to the brook, winding in and around the underbrush that lined the banks. Little animals scurried up and down the trees, like they were playing a devilishly clever game of tag with their friends, all the while ignoring the two humans that walked amidst them.

"You do know where you're going right?..." Aurora asked. The boy looked behind with eyebrows cocked.

"Yes, Milady. I know exactly where we are going."

"...Oh." She muttered quietly to herself, continuing her exploratory surveillance into the lives of the hypo energetic chipmunks and squirrels.

They soon came to a ford over the waters and crossed over into a new kind of forest where the trees grew to massive widths and heights. Needle like leaves the length of a person's for-arm hung from the blue pine branches, dancing in the wind that raced through the trees. The light became shrouded and the air filled with the scent of damp cedar and lavender buds. It was breathtakingly invigorating.

Aurora had to keep up with her guide who seemed unaffected by the surrounding splendour. She had so many questions to ask, but was afraid he might leave her behind out of tedium.

"You're not that much of a talker, are you?" He said with a smirk quite a ways up ahead. Aurora could feel the heat in her cheeks but realized that he was too far away to see.

"-Just trying to soak it all in..." She stated uneasily.

The boy nodded, waiting for some external acknowledgement of her inner toils and fears to emerge. Aurora released a shaky sigh and grounded herself to the idea that this whole event, might actually not be a dream.
"We might want to expedite our pace if we don't want to be caught out after nightfall..." He hinted as politely as he could manage. Aurora's face turned red and she quickly dug her eyes into the ground as they continued on in silence.

Hours passed and all that could be heard were the muffled sounds of the forest along with some random tune Aurora's companion was humming aloud. The trees then began to part and the sun shone through a clearing that spanned for at least a mile. The entire clearing was one big hill, with a lovely stone cottage perched atop it's crown. Tall grass lined the grounds, wafting in the late afternoon air, glistening in the setting sun.

A loud echoing growl cascaded through the space and surrounded the two. Wide eyed the boy looked at Aurora who had a bashful look on her face as she clutched her gullet. "Ahherm.... I'm hungry..." She muttered, face gone a deep shade of crimson. The boy tried his damnedest to muffle a laugh and motioned her onward to the cottage.

The building was vacant of life, vague marks from charring left behind on the walls and old furniture. The door groaned as it was caught in the wind. The sense of dread and pain hung upon each and every stone that remained behind. Aurora glanced into her companion's dull and lifeless eyes. She didn't have to ask why they were there.

"This was my home many years back..." he muttered complacently. Aurora nodded solemnly and stood there, uneasy and awkward.

"... Um... Excuse me?..." Aurora muttered quietly, her voice quaking in nervousness. The boy glanced over silently. "... How did I get here?"

He was taken aback by her question, noticing the vacant and expectant gaze in her eyes as she watched him pull out some food from his bag. Silence ensued, and Aurora began to wonder where all the food he was pulling out was coming from. There was a huge variety of vegetables and herbs, bread and cheese folded up nice and neatly in this tiny fold of fabric he carried on his back. Slowly he began to prep their supper, while Aurora stood beside the door twiddling her thumbs in anticipation of his answer.

"You can sit down, Lass." He said, motioning to a ragged chair to his right. "You're probably going to need to after what I tell ye." She obeyed without a second thought, plopping lightly down onto the rough rickety chair, almost falling through in the process.

His fingers quickly cut up the last of the carrots and tossed them into the pot perched atop a fire pit, awaiting to be lit.

"My name is Peregrith, son of Enslek and Adianna..." Red-hot fire began licking at the pot, making the broth dance and bubble from the heat near instantly. Aurora sat in silence. "People around here simply call me 'Pery'." He stated lightly as he handed her a bowl of what looked like slop.

Aurora glared at the concoction, her stomach growling hungrily yet again. Taking a deep breath and putting on her bravest face she swallowed down the first mouthful. Her taste buds were tingling with blandness, but she was hungry. Pery sat beside her on the bottom side of an old wooden bucket.

"You are in Avalon, Lass, a world apart from your own."

Aurora's mind froze. She knew that she wasn't home anymore, but to have it verbally confirmed just made it that much more mind numbing. Many things ran through her head at that moment, and the one big question that overshadowed all the rest poked through the internal babble, into the open silence around them.

"How am I going to get back?" She whispered to herself, more so than her companion. She glanced to Pery who sat there as still as a statue, eyes unable to make contact. Aurora knew what that meant; she had seen it countless times with her mother within the last couple of hard years. There was no hope in hell of her finding her way back.

The food in her belly threatened to revolt as she closed her eyes and took many deep, regulated breaths. It was a couple of minutes before she realized Pery was talking to her, trying to calm her from her little internal meltdown.

"One never knows in Avalon. There could most definitely be a way back to your world, I just... Kanna will know." He said at last, trying not to go into a panic himself. He wrapped a blanket around Aurora as she huddled next to the bristling fire. The blanket was warm; comforting... temporarily shielding her from her own racing emotions. Pery didn't know what to say to the girl he had so recently just met. He felt as if he should comfort her, but the action of reaching out to her scared him. What if she snapped and ran off? His objective would be null and void.

"There be fairies here..."He whispered comfortingly, trying to get past the tears that rolled down her cheeks. She looked up, eyes alive with a sudden rush of questions aching to be asked. "Magic and a wonderful world unlike anything you have ever seen..."

Aurora couldn't hold onto her thoughts any longer and let all the questions she had wondered since she had gotten there spew out in a ten question long sentence. Things like: How she had gotten into this dream-like world, what exactly those creatures were that had chased them, how he knew who she was right off the bat, and a whole matter of other questions that she barraged upon this oddly speaking boy.

Finally, when Aurora ran out of breath and Pery could open his mouth to answer, the comforting silence was interrupted by a loud crash within the surrounding trees.

Pery bolted up and dumped the stew on the cinders, leaving them to sizzle and hiss their objections. Wide eyed, Aurora muttered what the matter was. Pery instantly snapped his hand over her mouth as he glanced out the nearest window. To his horror, a very large beast, twice the size of those that pursued them this morning, came barrelling towards the hut, determined and ready to kill anything in its path.

"-Time to run again." He muttered breathlessly as he practically shoved Aurora out the back door and into the vast darkness that beheld the surrounding woods. Aurora's ears rang with the sound of her own heartbeat and laboured breath. Sheer terror melted through her veins, making her wish she had those answers to what was chasing them and why.

Her heart raced as the sound of their running footsteps crunching through last season's dried leaves seemed to echo eerily around them. The sound of the hut crumbling from the monster's angry blow reached their ears, making Pery skip a beat in stride as they tried to get as far away from there as they possibly could.

Even in the darkness, Aurora could see how crushed Pery was to have the only connection to his family being blasted to smithereens. He was so tempted to turn tale and kick that monster's face in for desecrating those stones, but thought better of it for fear of putting his companion in danger.

Pery and Aurora darted behind a huge tree the span of a spacious lavatory. Listening intently to anything that may be following, all they could hear was their own laboured breath.

"Why the hell are those things chasing us?" Aurora exclaimed in a whisper between breaths.

Pery glanced at her and turned away in embarrassment. "-I stole some things from them… Now they're out to kill me." He jeered sarcastically. Aurora gave him a look of annoyance as Pery shuffled from foot to foot.

"Oh my God, I'm following a delinquent thief..." Aurora mumbled to herself.

"It was a bunch of magical devices they had stolen from Kanna, Milady. They took a great amount of healing supplies that were meant for the towns-folk..."He said exasperated. "She's the *Seer* of the area; people come to her for spells and talismans against the evils of this world."

"Wait a minute, Seer? As in *hedgewitch*? As in a *witch-witch*?... and what kind of evil exactly? More of those monsters back there?"

"Each world has their balance of good and evil forces, Milady. Ours is no different."

"My world is different!"

"... I know there aren't much *magical* forces in your world, Aurora, but those that are dark within their soul are balanced with those that are light..."

Aurora stood there, blank-faced as slate. *Is he trying to pull some religious thing on me?* The inner debate of a balanced religion ran through her head as Pery silently began to walk further into the darkness that surrounded them. Aurora snapped out of her thoughts and stumbled through the underbrush as quietly as she could manage.

"Pery, wait- wait! I can't see.... Why are your eyes glowing?..." Her eyes bulged in the darkness. His eyes were glowing, as if reflecting light like a cat. Aurora's hair stood on end at the eerie sight of it.

"-Spell." He muttered patiently as he strode right in front of Aurora. She could feel Pery's hand glide over her face and had to step back from the sheer closeness that she was not used to; clearly to him, personal boundaries didn't mean much.

Within a couple of seconds, Aurora's vision became as clear as day. She could see everything with an eerie clarity that goes beyond the eye's sight.

"We must move fast. The Aslaik is still hunting us and this sight only lasts an hour…"

Aurora didn't have to be told. She kept up with her companion easily as they loped through the dank and crowded paths. She wasn't sure if she wanted to meet this Hedge witch that could, in all possibilities, change her into something unpleasant; If she knew *this* kind of magic, what else did this lady know?

Chapter
Four

The night stretched on forever as they made their way painstakingly through the winding trails. The little animals that came alive in the darkness of night, leaving an eerie glow to Aurora's eyes. They left blurred images in their wake as they scurried about the forest floor. The trees were never half as lively as they were at that moment.

Pery marched on, wordless and unaffected by the beauty that was around them. Aurora was looking everywhere but at her own feet, when she tripped over a root and landed firmly onto the leaf-strewn forest floor with a painful sounding thud. Shaking off the inner embarrassment and slight body ache, she glanced around for her companion, only to realize all she saw was darkness.

"-Pery… Peregrith!" Aurora whispered desperately, her heart trying to escape her chest. She grasped into thin air hoping to grasp hold of a branch or tree trunk to stabilize her as she stood. She jumped a foot as a hand firmly grasped hers to pull her up from the ground.

"No worries, Milady." Pery muttered soothingly. Aurora's fears settled as a little orb of light appeared in her palm. It was the size of a marble; glowing a soft blue and feeling as warm as a little kitten. Pery pulled out a similar orb that glowed a soft yellow in place of the blue. It seemed brighter than her dinky little light, producing a wonderful aura about him that gave Aurora the chills.

"Kanna gave me these to ward off night-creatures." He explained proudly as he jumped over a thin shallow stream. An uneasy feeling crept along Aurora's spine as she realized what he had meant. Out of the darkness appeared many sets of menacingly shining eyes, circling the two in hopes of finding a late night snack. Aurora shrank a little within herself as she stiffly kept on Pery's tail, refusing to so much as look at the monsters that loomed beyond the light.

"No worries, they can't touch us as long as we have these."

A small whimper squeaked from Aurora as they continued through the darkness with a pack of lord-knows-what following their every step. Hours passed without a word as morning larks began chirping merrily up in the trees. Aurora was exhausted, dragging her feet through everything, wishing that she had some more food in her belly than just a pathetic serving of poorly made stew. Her mind drifted back to her world where there was a secure stash of chocolate bars awaiting her amidst her things. Oh, how she wanted to shove a nice, thick, sweet Hershey bar into her face, the enigmatically euphoric taste melting on her tongue, and then was it down with a bottle of clear pop. Thank goodness Pery hadn't noticed her daydreaming as she wiped the slobber from her face; she was fairly positive she wouldn't be able to withstand the embarrassment.

"How far are we?" She drawled on in a half stupor. Pery remained silent as they climbed a steep hill, Aurora huffing from exhaustion and hunger. As they reached the crown and looked to what lay beyond, there was a gasp of awe as Aurora gazed upon the splendour of Kanna's house.

It was nothing like how she pictured it to be. It was a meadow-like clearing, with an ancient twisted tree as the focal point to which everything was based around. The house, which was round and lain with fist sized smooth stones. There were two small attachments at the back that mirrored the pattern of the main room with tear-shaped windows stained a very opaque sky blue. Each stone was a different colour of light pastel, to which an arm of ivy clutched possessively. From those stone walls spread a whole manner of plants, herbs that were most likely meant for potions and spells, and a vast variety of animals that pecked at the insects and munched on pesky weeds. All of this glorious wonder was nestled into a wicker fence that hugged the dear cottage and showed the border of the woman's domain to all that may venture.

Morning rays licked at the carved wooden door, illuminating it in the warmth that day had to offer. To Aurora's surprise, it swung open to someone that made the entire scene laughably complete.

"-Peregrith, my lad!" The woman bellowed with soft glee. Pery smiled back and sauntered down the little path to the open arms that welcomed him. The woman was old and round, the way a wise woman should look in any mystical realm. She wore a lilac purple shiv that was wrapped with a multicoloured apron. Her hair was a long fiery fury of orange and silver, twisted into braids atop her head, framing large eyes as blue as ice. As Aurora nervously approached the woman, she noticed that the woman didn't look at her as she crept closer. A moment of realization hit Aurora square upside the head when she came to realize the woman was very much blind.

"Kanna, I've brought you someone to meet..." Pery said calmly, motioning to Aurora who was involuntarily cowering behind a nearby shrub; she hadn't been this scared to meet someone since her mom forced her to shake Dracula's hand when she was six at the typically cheesy theme park.

The woman held out her hand as if grasping in to thin air. Aurora gulped loudly and, understanding the frantic, wordless signals Pery was giving her to say something, let out a little squeak of a 'Hello' that no one had herd except herself. Finally after a couple moments passed, she braved her fears and took the lady's rough and wrinkled hand. Pery eased up a bit, eyes rolling dramatically at Aurora's cowardess. Kanna smiled sweetly and quietly laughed to herself as she led the girl inside, Pery following closely behind.

The house was a large greenhouse, with a small bed, table and cooking pit shoved over to one side. Birds flew in and out as they pleased, twirling around and chirping over Aurora's head as she gawked at the splendour. Hanging woven baskets of vines and flowers were strewn everywhere, bees and butterflies buzzing from each plant to the next. Curiosity soon overshadowed the fear and Aurora couldn't help but touch one of the more exotic flowers she had never seen before. A small runner vine snapped at her fingers just as she was about to touch the blossom, making her stagger back a few feet from surprise.

Her eyes snapped over to Pery who had seen the whole thing and was trying not to laugh as best he could.
"… So what is your name child?" Kanna said patiently, smirking at Pery who was now clutching his side, trying not to tumble over.

"Aurora." She said, as clearly as she could muster. Kanna stood there, staring at the place where Aurora would be. Aurora was confused as to why her name forced such awe onto the faces that heard it; beginning to wonder what importance it held in this world. The lady remained speechless as Aurora stood there awkwardly, wanting to tumble upon a comfy bed and sleep for days.

"Kanna…" Pery interjected softly, "May we have shelter here? Aslaiks were everywhere on the way here and we are close to being spent."

Kanna nodded firmly and motioned towards the left doorway in the rear of the room. "-Of course, my dear… I will prepare food for you." She stated more to Aurora than Pery.

Aurora shook the woman's odd reaction from her thoughts as she followed her young companion into the small room which held nothing more than a slim bed and a chair. The room seemed out of place with the lack of plants and little garden creatures, instead there was a shelf filled to the brim with crystals and shells of various sizes.

Neither hesitated a single step as they piled onto the wonderfully comfortable looking surfaces and both heavily sighed in unison.

"So are you gonna tell me who you guys think I am here?" Aurora muttered to Pery, as he stifled a yawn. The boy grunted lazily and settled himself in the large chair at the foot of the bed.

"-After sleep." He mumbled, closing his eyes. She wanted to shake the questions out of him, patience was never her virtue, but decided against it as she couldn't force her eyes open any longer; giving way to her nagging exhaustion. If she was lucky, maybe they would tell her something when she had more energy for insisting.

Chapter
Five

Aurora woke with the sun shining through the window brightly onto her face. She felt stiff and weak as she glanced towards the chair at the foot of the bed. It lay there vacantly absent of Pery. In his place was a bundle of cloth, neatly tucked and folded with a pair of shoes on top.

"Best change dearest." Came a booming voice from the other room, startling Aurora into next week. "If anyone came lookin' for ye, ye would be less conspicuous in those there."

She hesitated for a moment, thinking of who would come looking for her and why. With a shrug she set aside her confused curiosity and put on the cloths before her. It was a maroon long sleeved dress, plain in form with bits of embroidery on the sleeves and neck. It seemed worn but was almost a perfect fit as she admired herself in a round mirror she had missed hours before. Letting down her hair into tumbles of wavy curls, she reminded herself of a damsel in distress from some cheesy King Arthur movie, only without the bad acting and lame backdrops. Her stomach began rumbling ferociously, snapping her out of her little medieval day dream and making her clutch at her stomach with pain; hunger pains were annoying.

"Foods almost ready Milady…" Kanna bellowed as Aurora peaked out of her little room. It seemed to just be her and the old woman in the house, Pery was nowhere to be found. Kanna handed her a bowl filled with chunks of bread, cheese, meat and what looked like pink broccoli all neatly arranged in clumps of deliciousness. Aurora's mouth watered and she was almost drooling on the food as the intoxicating smells taunted her senses. As soon as Kanna handed her a fork, she was at it like there was no tomorrow. Within minutes the bowl was clean, Aurora smirking contently as she stood there patting her full belly. Kanna chuckled heartily as she polished off the rest of hers.

"-Where did Pery disappear to?"

"Oh, he's out hunting with Thom." Kanna stated dismissively as she scanned Aurora with her wise, seemingly unseeing eyes. "So you really are her then? You are Aurora." The woman stated rhetorically.

"-Aurora Clanilla." She replied, unsure of why it mattered so much. "From planet Earth…" She mumbled.

The hut boomed with laughter with the old woman wiping the tears from her wrinkled eyes. "Oh my dear, we're still on Earth, silly! This is Avalonia, not some alien planet! Ha ha hah…" Aurora could feel her face going bright red as she gazed at the woman almost hysterically laughing at her. "I'm surprised Pery didn't tell you about Avalonia."

"Believe me I've asked, he isn't very talkative though…" Aurora mumbled sadly. Kanna sat there smiling, her old-womanly wisdom obviously getting something Aurora had missed. "-I would very much appreciate someone telling me how I got here in the first place…"

The old woman sighed inwardly and looked into Aurora's curious eyes, holding her gaze to relay the seriousness of the matter.

"… Avalon is what you would call a *spirit world*, or more specifically *your* spirit world; The souls of your world enter through one of eleven gates, sprinkled all over the realm, and are born as various creatures and plants here. You see Aurora, this world and your world balance upon a fine tipped pedestal; if there are more souls within one world than the other, both worlds will become unbalanced and fall…

Only immortals and a few half-bloods are able to pass through the gate while still in their material state. Within those bloodlines are the *Precipitus* whom, if I'm not mistaken, would be your grandmother and therefore yourself."

Aurora stood there speechless. What the hell was this lady trying to tell her? That somehow her family was part of this world, yet part of hers as well? That these odd laws of passage applied to her entire bloodline? Meaning her mother as well? A painful knot appeared in her stomach as she ran all these questions threw her head.

Is this why Pery didn't talk about it? Who the hell am I to these people...

"You, Aurora are the last of the royal blood, and are the heiress to the Realm of Avalonia..." Kanna stated bluntly.

With those words, Aurora's thoughts broke. Everything she had guessed, everything she had wondered came to a halt with that one simple sentence. Each word went through her head with Aurora trying to decipher what they could mean. She was the last of her family... a family of which ruled over these strange lands; Lands to which she had never been. How is it she had not known about all of this?

Aurora clutched her chest, gasping desperately for the air that seemed thick and sludgy. Her thoughts snapped back to her mother as she fell clumsily to her knees; the great secret that her mother held from her. Was it to protect her, or selfishly bar her from this haven of magic? Suddenly, all Aurora wanted was to hold her mother close; to have her protect her only daughter from the mind boggling truth. Tears began to fall as Aurora quickly moved to hide her face.

"-How do I go back..." She spoke quietly, voice quivering from shock. A hand was placed gently upon her shoulder, making her cringe from such close contact. She felt so alone within this world. Even with Kanna and Pery there, she still felt empty and abandoned.

"... That's the trick my dear, there is no man made magic in all of Avalonia that can reverse the gate's path. Only an immortal or those of the blood can pass between the veil, and no one alive today knows how your bloodline does it."

Aurora couldn't take it any longer and bolted out of the hut, racing back the way she had come with as much speed as her legs could muster. The truth was too much, weighing down upon her chest like lead as she ran from herself more than her surroundings. Her ears pounded the sound of her heartbeat as gusts of wind brushed up against her face. With her mind spinning and her feet barely able to keep up with her, she tumbled over roots and branches, leaving bloody gashes and scratches upon her flesh. Hopelessness overtook her as she realized she was probably never going to go home. Cursing God and all manners of self loathing creatures, she resigned herself to die in this sick and depraved dark world she was now part of.

She remained lying in the woods for what felt like hours, listening to the faint echoes of Kanna's pleas in the distance. Her soul felt numb and her body an empty shell, cold and painless. Soon Aurora didn't feel that terrible urge to go home, she lost all inclination to exist at all within this world or her own. There was no way she would survive here and saw absolutely no point in trying.

Twilight engulfed the trees around her and she lulled in and out of a hallucinogenic dream. She kept hearing voices around her, unintelligible at first. They eventually became discernable from the sounds of the forest around her, saying that '*she should not give up so quickly*' and to '*be brave in the face of fear*'. Things her mom had always told her whenever she had tried something new. '*Don't be such a pussin wuss, it's not like you're dead yet.*' Was the loudest voice that woke Aurora from her stupor, it reminded her eerily of her Grandmother the last time she had visited as a child. A chill ran down her spine as she stiffly sat up.

Peering through the trees, the evening peaking with night, Aurora glanced at a shadow that slowly approached her. Part of her wanted to run, yet she convinced herself to remain still; the figure was of someone she had come to rely on in such a short period of time. An orb of blue light glowed in front of the silhouette as it stepped closer.

"Aurora…" Pery called out with relief as he knelt next to her. He scanned her torn and mud laden body, "Are you injured?"

"… M-my ankle." Is all that escaped her dry and scratchy throat. Carefully gathering the girl about her waist, Pery hoisted Aurora up to her feet, steadying her as she slowly regained her strength.

"P-Pery, I'm so bloody scared of this new place… I… don't know what I'm going to do…" She whispered tensely as a column of tears escaped down her face.

"You would be a fool not to be scared of change…" He muttered softly, "Especially in your circumstances… but you shouldn't let that fear rule your life. You have one chance to live the life you have now, Milady. Many don't get that opportunity…"

Aurora winced, cringing from the pain as they slowly made their way back down the path to Kanna's.
"And as for not knowing what to do about this whole situation, there is more to your story than you know. Before you decide on anything, I think you should know the rest… And whatever you may decide, know that I will be there to help…"

Aurora couldn't help but smile a little. Through the last couple of days, this boy has carried her, soldier like, through the most elegant, beauteous, freaky, hell-hole she had ever been in. Even if she does die a most horrible and gruesome death, which she had no doubt would happen eventually in this place- at least with Peregrith's help, she wouldn't die of helplessness before the week was through.

Chapter
Six

Kanna's eyes lit up as Pery wobbled towards the hut, clutching Aurora protectively to prevent her from falling. The woman babbled on about how worried she was and how her son had gone looking for the both of them while they were dallying. A tall muscular man popped his head out of the other bedroom as Pery sat Aurora securely on a chair. The man, seeming to be in his late thirties, goggled at Aurora from behind the many plants whipping about within the hut. His grey speckled hair reminded Aurora of an old porcupine perched atop the man's head, his sausage lips pressed into a think line as he looked on.

"Thom, don't just stand there- give us a hand!" Kanna cried impatiently as she began massaging Aurora's foot with a handful of vile smelling goop. The man jumped from his hidey hole and leapt across the room, quickly gathering a bundle of cloth strips from a small box. Darting the snapping vines that seemed to detest his closeness to them, Thom jumped back to Aurora's ankle, wrapping it as swiftly and gently as one would a newborn babe. It surprised her that someone with so much bulging muscle could be so nimble with his fingers.

Within a couple of minutes, Aurora was sitting comfortably in front of a little pit fire, leg placed carefully upon a smooth trunk stool. The rest of her company seemed intertwined in a deep and interesting conversation about Thom's winter work. Apparently, every fall he would go to the mines to the north-east, and every spring he would return with not only money from the gold he had mined, but various small jewels every worker was permitted to keep. The three of them *OOOed* and *AAAWWed* over the shiny gems the size of the man's thumb. As beautiful as the gems were, Aurora didn't care to listen as to what Thom was saying so vehemently about the vast properties those stones possessed. She was simply glad that their eyes weren't upon her at the moment.

While she gazed outside into the night, little glowing lights began dancing about the garden that surrounded the hut. When she was young, Aurora used to think they were fairies, going to and from work on protecting their little homes. Since her discovery of fireflies however, her belief in magical creatures have been outgrown. Even without magical creatures about, Aurora could almost feel how magical this new world was.

It was odd how all of her fear had melted away when Pery had found her. She couldn't tell if she was forming a crush on this kind and wild boy, or if it was just a huge amount of faith she placed in his helping her. At that moment she had made up her mind that the only way she was to get home, was to do what she was sent here for.

"So what exactly is the rest of my story?" She said calmly. Everyone stopped and whirled around to look at her, jaws almost dropping to the floor. Evidently, they had all thought about how to approach the delicate subject without making her run off again; bewildered that she would bring it up herself.

"W-well…" Kanna stuttered, still slightly shocked.

"You already know about your heritage, am I correct M'Lady?" Pery asked delicately, an odd smile lingering on his lips. Aurora nodded slowly, waiting patiently with a large knot twisting at her guts. "The Queen, your Grandmother, had made an enemy of Isietha, whom once held control over the northern dominion. The Queen had waged war and raised claim to the northern lands. The battle was won and Isietha's army defeated, though in Isietha's hatred for our Queen, her spirit remained in this world, refusing to cross over until your bloodline is wiped from this world… Isietha is pure darkness, and threatens this world with her new army of Aslaiks and other creatures of putrification…"

"-But there be a *Harbenger of Life* that the Mistress of Air fortold to yer Grandmother before she vanished." Kanna interjected. "This harbenger will defeat Isietha at her own game and raise de army to beat all armies... an' at this army's head, will be the *Goddess of Dawn* wielding the realm's fate!"

Kanna finished with a sigh and a happy expression on her tired lips, her unseeing eyes gazing into the space of emptiness.

"... There's one problem with this prophesy..." Aurora muttered exuberantly. "I am definitely not a goddess... or any kind of deity that I can think of. Plus, I'm pretty sure I can't control any form of fate except for my own-If I can even do that much..."

Aurora's hopeless expression began to mirror that of those around the room. Only Pery had his emotions closely masked within himself. She looked into his glorious soft wild-green eyes and tried to find some knowledge within them that the other two wasn't sharing. Then she found it. The knowledge and strength that she was hoping for, shining brightly upon her. He knew exactly who she was, even if she didn't.

"Trust me M'Lady, in the end you will be..." Thom said plainly. Silence hummed through the room, the only sounds being from the crackle of the fire, even the insects in the flowers remained silent. "Everyone knows of your coming; they've been expecting it for eons. The one thing no one accounted for was that you would be this young..."

Aurora stared at him, a look of confused bewilderment written all over her face.

"All the people I've spoken with, half expected you to be on the wiser side... Like Mama, here-" A loud smack echoed across the room as Kanna smacked her son with a flame-fan.

"Ye, mean old! Boy if I was you, I'd keep me mouth shut 'bout me age!"

"-Ma I meant nothin' of it…" Thom exclaimed, muttering the same country bumpkin accent as his mother.

His mother glared at him, looking as though she would wallop him if it weren't for the pleasant company. Thom shied away from her blind glare. If it weren't for Aurora's knowledge of Kannas blindness, she would've never guessed She had no mortal sight.

"What I meant M'Lady, was that being young is a great advantage. While people are looking for someone *My Mother's Age,*" Thom said teasingly, ignoring his mother's waving fist. "you will be remotely safe from the enemy's gaze."

Aurora's face lit up with realization; she was in slightly less danger than she had initially thought. The thought of all those Aslaiks that had nearly caught her and Pery quickly resurfaced and the little spurt of hope that appeared just a moment ago, quickly vanished. But the fact that they weren't looking for *her* made her a little happy. It still raised the question as to what she was supposed to do to help against this scary-as-hell ghostly enemy.

"The only way to stop Isietha is to acquire the 5 fates from the mistressess of the elements." Pery stated, bursting through Aurora's inner thoughts. "The rest of the prophecy states that darkness cannot be destroyed, but it can be banished using 5 elements found in nature. You, Aurora, were sent here to claim these 5 fates, elements that only those of your bloodline can lay claim to, and combine them to banish Isietha and her army from our world."

Aurora stared at Pery, unblinking and barely breathing. *'This is why I'm here; to be a go-fetch-it dog to the gods? Well, crap…'* She thought vehemently to herself. With evil seeming to loom on these people's doorstep, she didn't have the heart to say no… though she couldn't help but think a few choice explicit words to whatever higher power was listening.

"Ok…." She said at last.

"… Ok?" They all repeated in unison.

"Ok, I'll do it."

The three of them gasped, unable to think of what to say.

"-I'm warning you though, I'm probably gonna be gutted before I come close to reaching the first… whatever it is." She muttered dully. All three burst into smiles and began telling stories about the wild and wonderful things they've experienced and seen on their travels. Tall tales of giants and winged horses, golems and angels littered each story with adventure and fear. Aurora's eyes became heavy and before she knew it, she was sleeping soundly in the wake of the coal's flickering flames.

✦━━━━━━━━━━✦

She woke to the morning larks **chirping** their sweet melody, the suns rays gently caressing the hut to bid good morrow. Unwrapping herself from the blanket of furs someone had lain upon her sometime during the night, she rose from the lumpy bed, moving towards the light that warmed her spirit. The outer world was alive with their hustle and bustle of everyday life. The bees were pollinating, the birds were singing, frogs were croaking, crickets playing, and Kanna stood in the midst of it all, tending her garden of healing. The old woman reminded Aurora of what a Grandmother should be: gentle yet stern, knowledgeable yet almost painfully blunt. The girl couldn't help but smile at the immense difference between this woman and her own grandma, who was all too proper and scornful. She wondered if it was because of the grandmother's duties to this realm; did it make her hard and uptightedly proper?

"Good morrow, M'Lady." Pery called from behind palm leaves as Aurora slowly stepped from her room. He was shoving things from the food pantry into a large sack, muttering something Aurora couldn't understand while doing it. Kanna strode into the hut with a basket full of herbs and flowers, giving Aurora a quick smile as she moved towards an odd looking table covered in dried leaves. Thom,

Aurora had noticed, was outside in the warmth of a beautiful spring day using his bulging muscles to chop log after log of fire wood. Feeling fidgety and awkward from not having a task at hand, Aurora slowly strolled outside to walk the paths that wound around the house and garden.

The sweet and spicy scents wafting from the plants soothed Aurora's nerves as she watched a pair of fox pups play 100 yards off passed the wicker fence. In the shade of an apple tree she sat, gazing at the scene before her. The path was lain with small, flat, chalky white stones the size of her fist and twisted here and there, making swirled patterns all through the clearing. A little hutch for fowl was set up at the far right, along with a secure pen housing two pot-bellied piglets and an old bleeting goat with her kid. To the left, near the rear of the hut was a cove that kept the fire wood dry. Beside that was a small hill with an oval door placed upon the flat side facing Aurora, which was most likely the root cellar.

After a short time, Aurora found herself nodding off from slight boredom. She wasn't used to not having to do anything and was starting to regret knowing she was a blue-blood in this curiously new world. Unconsciously, her feet led her to the animal pen, the pigs grunted loudly at her for disturbing their sunning in their muck. Her hands carefully patted the mother goat's head as it tried grabbing at any bit of clothing that was close enough to chew.

"I believe Lady likes ye Princess..."Called a deep voice a few feet away. Aurora nearly jumped out of her skin as she snapped her gaze towards the voice. Thom sat in the shade against a willow's trunk, looking at her in amusement. Aurora snapped her hand back to her sides, eyes falling to her feet as her skin shone a brilliant crimson.

"O-oh, I.... forgot... you...were..." She mumbled, petering off into an awkward silence.

"No worries Miss!" Thom exclaimed exuberantly. "You probably have plenty in your head there-begin your pardon for my bluntness- but I've noticed that most decent people born into rank, wish for somethin' more common…"

Aurora had to smile at that. She knew he was right, even though she hadn't even had that rank for very long.

"If ye have a hankerin' to do somethin', yer free to collect the goose eggs over yonder. The basket is hangin' on that hook on the side…"

Aurora was thrilled to have something to do other than wait and twiddle her thumbs. Within five minutes she had fetched the eggs and brought them back to Thom, who then handed her a fistful of rubbery carrots. Feeding the mama goat Thom called '*Lady*' wasn't her idea of chores, but it did help alleviate the knot that had formed tightly in her gut.

Kanna called out to her and Thom for lunch when the sun reached high noon, which was lucky for Aurora, because the growls of her stomach had frightened the little goat kid off to the other side of the pen. After a meal of spiced soup and meat tarts, all four lounged in front of the fire pit, ready for an afternoon nap.

"Well, you two are pretty much set." Kanna stated calmly, nodding to the bags that sat beside the door. "Everything that can be spare is there, and I pray to the goddess that she will protect you…" She muttered, voice trailing off sadly. Even though it was not in any form a dismissal, Pery stood and gathered the two bags, tossing them both over his shoulders. As much as she didn't want to leave yet, Aurora knew that the longer she put it off, the harder it would be to go. She cleared her throat as she stood and looked at the two strangers that had become almost like family, no words could express the feelings that clung to her chest.

Before she could make a move to the door, Kanna stood before her, placing a small trinket in her hands, clasping the young girl's with her ancient wrinkled fingers. Kanna looked directly at Aurora, holding fast a gaze that reflected another world. Reality quickly faded away and brought her to a land of water and forests cloaked in the light of the setting sun. There were two silhouettes in the background, holding hands and looking upon one another as lovers would. The scene melted towards them in one fluid motion, stopping a foot away from the lovers. The woman looked familiar in her side view, an image that had once haunted Aurora's thoughts in her dreams. Upon closer inspection, the woman reminded her very much of Emily's, possibly in the woman's youth years prior. The man seemed wild and unkempt, though elegant with the status of noble blood coursing through the man's veins. The man gently touched a pendant that hung from his lover's neck, a clear pendant with silver etchings and a garnet encased upon its upper-base. The pendant glowed upon her skin, shining of the magic it held within, making Aurora transfixed within her gaze.

Shine upon the light of truth. Let it guide you through the mysts that blind remissly thrown askew.

Aurora's world snapped back to her as the sight of the lovers faded from her eyes. The words that echoed throughout her thoughts, fell short of understanding as she went over them in her head. Opening her hand to reveal her prize, she realized the same pendant that hung from the woman in the vision sat pleasantly within her palm. It seemed warm within her grasp, charged with some puzzling form of an invisible shield.

"I hope you find yourself, Aurora… and I pray for your protector." Kanna whispered, a tear rolling down her weathered face. "Bid you merry meet Peregrith…" She muttered sadly as she clutched him in a firm embrace, Pery clutching firmly back. "And I bid you farewell, sweet girl." The woman embraced Aurora in much the same way as Pery before releasing them both from her grasp.

With a final fair well from Kanna and a muffled goodbye from Thom, the two set off from the little cottage of Eden, into the vast wilderness that lay ahead. Even though Aurora still had no idea what she was doing, nor what she was actually supposed to do, she had faith that whatever had brought her here in the first place, might just take pity on her and protect her from her own ignorance and stupidity.

Chapter Seven

The late afternoon sky threatened rain as they travelled northward through the thicket of willow. They followed the river as they had before, taking care to stay off the roads and keep to the wildlife trails that kept close to the areas only source of water. Deer would be seen drinking at the banks from behind the trees; peaceful and elegant, gracefully beautiful.

The first handful of hours left Aurora tired, bored, and slightly lost. Normally she would look at which side of a tree the moss would grow to find due north, but each tree either had no moss on it at all, or it was covered from tip to root in the stuff. Within the last half hour, she had caught herself dancing to silent songs playing through her head, receiving odd looks more than once from Pery who walked a few paces ahead of her.

That night they had camped out in the middle of nowhere it seemed. Every tree looked identical from the last and the creek seemed to wind on forever. Aurora was content to sleep on a mossy forest floor with a small camp fire at her feet and a large serving of leftover stew from Kanna's. Pery wrapped a thick cloak around her as she was slowly and unwillingly falling asleep. All Aurora could remember before sleep had taken her into another world, was the soft angelic melody that floated through the woods.

Aurora woke suddenly to a crashing sound on her immediate left. She bolted up from her moss bed as a wild boar came crashing down upon the place she had been laying, not three seconds prior, a bolt jutting from it's twitching neck. Pery stood a few feet away, clutching some odd kind of crossbow weapon tightly in his hands.

"Blasted-hell, I didn't get you did I?!" Pery exclaimed loudly. Aurora leaned against the nearest tree, trying to get her heart pumping again as Pery moved to drag the large lump of wild pig into the trees. Begrudgingly she sluffed it off and slowly threw a small bundle of dead logs onto the warm coals by her feet. The air was chilly and damp, she could almost feel the rain misting down upon her hair as she wrapped her cloak around her properly. The thing was heavy, but not as thick as it should be in Aurora's mind. She tried to ignore the grotesque smell of gutted animal as she prodded the fire awake with a long wet stick.

"So what's our first destination *Trail Master*?" She called out to Pery, her voice sarcastic and filled with the longing for more sleep. She glanced back instinctively and immediately had wished that she hadn't. The fur of the beast lay in a neat pile beside the hunk of meat, innards lay in a pile on the other side, and there was Pery, carving the hunks of flesh quickly and skilfully with nothing more than a small dagger. It was so unnerving to watch such a terror of a boar be resorted to meat and flesh within such a short time. Aurora wanted to toss her cookies so terribly bad.

"Meridarch is another full day's walk from here. Meat and hides will fetch a fair sum." He said, face guarded from laughing at her twisted expression. Pery began rubbing some sort of powder onto the meat and the underside of the fur, tying both up in a large sack and hoisting it up on his shoulders. "... Sorry MiLady, but you will have to carry our provisions..." He stated abashed. Aurora just shrugged and threw the last remaining bag over her own shoulder, almost toppling over from the weight.

"-What on earth do you have in here?" Aurora muttered exasperated as she steadied herself and waited as Pery kicked out the hungrily burning fire. He shrugged nonchalantly and disappeared into the trees for a moment, coming back with full water-bladders in hand. The nip of the early morning beginning to give way to the sunny day that lay ahead. The trail they followed remained the same as they wound their way through the thick forest.

As the creek began twisting west, they crossed at a shallow point, taking care not to get the baggage wet. Aurora hiked up her dress as far as she dared as she waded through the water, Pery marching straight through with no care or worry of getting wet.

The day pressed on as they left the safety of the stream and continued due north, only stopping for short breaks and quick meals. Time dragged on for Aurora as boredom began to overtake her senses.

"What does a person do out here… other than walk and not speak to who ever they're travelling with?" She hinted bluntly.

A boom of a laugh burst forth as Pery shook his head in humour. "Most people do not travel with company unless they're family…" He stated while trying to repress a giggle and failing miserably. "So whatever families talk about is what they do, I suppose. I've always travelled alone..."

Aurora fell silent, pondering over what people may think of two young adults travelling the country together. Would people mistake them for lovers? It gave her chills thinking about it. She had never had a boyfriend, let alone a lover…

"If anyone asks, you're my sister… -Ashlin." He muttered, deep in thought. Evidently he was thinking exactly what she was and was trying to make an alias for her from thin air. "You have been missing for years and had finally found your only living relative. You were raised way yonder, north of the mountain lines when you herd of my were-abouts and came to see me. All anyone needs to know at this point is that I'm bringing you back north." He said at last.

"… Do I really have to be an Ashlin?" Pery turned to look at her, confusion written all across his face.
"It's just that Ashlin… sounds too… I don't know-ashy…"

He hid a smirk as he thought it over, "What would you suggest then Milady? People will know it's you if you use your own name-"

"Oh I know!" Aurora muttered quickly, "I just don't care for the name... What about Rose or Roslen..."

"How about Aury... that's common enough in these parts." He stated as they came to yet another fork in the trail. Pery veered right without a beat and began humming a little melody to himself.

"How is it that you know this trail?" Aurora asked quietly.

"-Most people take these trails when moving from town to town when walking. It's more secure than taking the road that's meant for those with more cargo." He stated briskly. "It's a common means of travel for wild beasts as well, oddly enough."

"Like deer...?"

"Yeh, and boars such as the one I found this morning-"

"That scared the shit out of me I'd have you know...!" Aurora stated heavily, annoyed by the large grin across Pery's face. "It's not funny!"

Pery kept his mouth shut firm, trying hard not to burst into another round of laughter.

They continued on through the afternoon and into the evening, right up to the deep blue that twilight offered at days end. The pack carried by Aurora was no longer heavy, though her feet ached something fierce. She no longer cared about the surrounding forest and all its inhabitants, only about the thought of having a glorious bed in which to sleep.
Mindlessly she trekked on behind Pery, not realizing that he had halted until she nearly ran into him. Peeking over his shoulder, Aurora noticed a bunch of little lights glowing half a mile down in a small valley

straight ahead. From the tree line where the two stood, she could see that the small town was nestled comfortably within a ten foot wall of stone and logs. It stretched around the little buildings within, guarding it from any foe that dare try and overtake it. The trail that Pery and her were on, became a small stone path that led through the fields surrounding the town.

Pery turned to her and quickly put the hood up over Aurora's head. "Keep your head down and don't speak unless necessary… we really don't need people knowing that you've come back until we have to." He said forcefully. Aurora nodded wordlessly, mind set on looking as meek as humanly possible, which wasn't all that hard.

They marched down the stone path, through the fields of vegetables and grains, and before Aurora knew it, they were standing in front of a door to the left of the main gate. With a couple of quick words from Pery, the two were permitted entry and allowed to roam.

The shops were closed and people were scarce. Aurora kept to what she was told and didn't speak a word as they moved towards a large double floored tavern at the corner of the last street. It was beginning to be cold and dank, gloomy penniless slobs lined the coveys of each shop, huddled within themselves for warmth. A pang of pity grabbed Aurora's guts and twisted as she moved to give them money like she would have at home. She reached for her pockets and realized that she too was penniless and homeless. Never had she thought that it would happen to her.

A door marked with the words Panther across the frame soon stood before them, the thoughts of gloom and despair drifting off as they entered the cheery building. Pery strode forward towards the bar on the left, Aurora following close behind like a lost little duckling. The tender of the bar, a big burly man about seven feet tall with a girth to match twirled around and grunted, his long red beard flopping with his mouth.

"Wha kin I geh Yah?" The man boomed at Pery, completely disregarding Aurora to her unfathomable relief.

"Good evening Panther," Pery said affectionately, a grin slowly forming across his tight lips. "My sis and I need a room."

The man looked at him with a curious expression, then at Aurora who still looked at the floor. A look of understanding crossed the man's face as he slid a key across the stained counter. "… Haven't seen ye in years, Pery." The man muttered quietly, so only they could hear, "The usual room. Be sure to sit and talk after the crew be gone." Peregrith nodded and moved to run up the narrow stairway to their left. Aurora glanced at the nearest patron and saw a thin fragile looking old woman glaring at them as if they were the devil's spawn. Snapping her eyes away, Aurora sped up to Peregrith and disappeared into the room, shutting the door firmly behind her.

With only one bed in the little creaky room, Aurora hurdled off her cloak, took two tiny steps and flung herself on the insanely uncomfortable bed. "I call dibs!" She exclaimed wildly, heaving a big sigh from the relaxation the bed had promised.

"Of course MiLady." He muttered sarcastically, sitting lightly on the bed.

Aurora turned to her side and watched casually as her companion stared mindlessly out the small dusty window.

"What's up, Peregrith?" Aurora mumbled uneasily.

He glanced at her for a brief moment and in that moment, she could swear that the look of pain in his eyes had mirrored that of her mothers. The kind of pain that holding a secret allows. "… Nothing." He said after composing himself.

There was a swift knocking at the door and not a split second later, a petite fiery middle-aged woman came bursting into the room. "Pery, my sweet! I've longed te be with ye ever since ye lef-" The woman stopped cold in her tracks, balancing a tray of food in one hand and a pitcher of ale in the other as she stood goggling at Aurora lying on the bed. The woman's eyes widened to the size of dinner plates and her mouth kept opening and closing like a fish out of water. Peregrith looked at the woman and back at Aurora, and couldn't speak any more than the woman could.

"I-I'm Aury…" Aurora stuttered nervously, "H-his sister."

The woman snapped her head to Peregrith, eyes narrowing to slits. "You don't have a sister, Pery!"

"Now, Liza calm-"

"Could have told me she was your bride! That you had found someone else- Pery for the Goddesses sake I saved myself for you-"

"Liza, we are NOT married, nor are we ever going to get married-"

"Your mistress then- she's your mistress"

"Eliza, calm your fool head and sit the Hell down! I will explain if you will be calm!" Peregrith stated impatiently, teeth audibly grinding down to a pulp. Liza looked at Aurora with a dark hateful glare. Putting down the food and drink with a loud and disruptive thud, she crossed to the foot of the bed, leaned against the wall and crossed her arms in distrust. Aurora couldn't help but feel a little sick from the evil glare the fiery woman sent her way.

"… Alright… Explain" The woman muttered curtly, turning the gaze on him next.

"Ok," Peregrith began patiently, making sure to speak extra clearly as though he were talking to a half-wit. "Do you remember that job I told you about a long time ago?"

Liza's face turned as blank as a clean sheet of paper. She had no idea.

"-The one where I was to guide an old hag around Avalonia…?" Liza's eyes lit up in recognition, but the hateful doubt returned as she laid her eyes upon Aurora; pretty and definitely not an old hag. "The job changed a bit." He muttered quietly, making Liza look at him inquisitively.

"Alright…"Liza said slowly, unsure if she could take him for his word. "So what does that mean for -Us…?"She muttered enticingly. Peregrith turned away silently, looking back out the window again.

"-I see…" She spoke gently, turning towards the door, motioning to leave. "If you need a- a friend or some lovin' , I'll be here…" Without a second glance Liza was out of the room, leaving it empty and the air heavy.

Aurora glanced at her companion and waited; he refused to talk about it. "Get some sleep, Princess…"Was all he managed to say before he left the room all in a hurry. Aurora had a chilling feeling that something was up with Peregrith; that things weren't all he let on. She lay curled up on the bed, her cloak wrapped around her securely and wanted nothing more than to drift into an uncomfortable sleep in what might be their last chance for a warm Inn. Ignoring her rumbling stomach and easing her muscles from the million mile hike of that day, she fell asleep faster than she could blink it away.

Chapter
Eight

The building was too quiet; making Aurora's ears ring as she groggily rose from the warmth of her bed. To her surprise Peregrith wasn't in the room yet, making her wonder if he was getting drunk downstairs with Liza, maybe he took her up on that offer after all. It made her shiver a bit at the thought, and a sliver of jealousy emerged out of nowhere that made Aurora question how much sleep she had actually received. She shook her head and opened the thick door to the hall which, even though she tried her damnedest to be quiet, every floorboard gave way to even the slightest amount of pressure, making her cringe with every stiff movement.

Leaning over the railing, she gazed curiously to the floor where she immediately spotted Peregrith and the barman by the fire. The rest of the place was deserted, and made the scene in front of her almost picturesque to something you would see in a good movie. Swiftly wrapping her cloak around her and placing the hood over her head she declined down the stairs, preparing to flee back to the safety of her room if some drunken slob decides to jump out and grab her.

She didn't have to worry about it at all as she could hear loud rasping and snoring coming out of every other room she passed, they were even louder than the floorboards. In the shadows Aurora crept until the light of the fire just hit her cloak and there she waited, too nervous to go any further.

"Ye can come over, Aurora." Spoke a very low and quiet voice, making Aurora's eyes widen in surprise. An equally quiet and low voice rumbled and chuckled through the main floor as startlement faded into understanding. He must've known all along.

Hesitantly, Aurora strolled over and stood between the two staring nonchalantly into the fire. Peregrith darted off and came back with a chair faster than Aurora could blink, shocking her so much that she stumbled back and fell into the chair with a loud and sloppy thud.

"Pery, ye shouldn't do that to eh lady…" The man frowned disapprovingly, making Peregrith shrink away slightly with regret. A couple moments passed between the two, silence only filled by the crackle of the fire and far off sounds of patrons dreaming.

"Panther, we need a map." Peregrith stated hopelessly.

"Do ye mean te tell me, Pery, that you set out on this quest without knowin a fathem as to where ye are supposed to go…?" Peregrith just nodded as this man glared at him in disapproval. Peregrith was abashed and by the colour of his cheeks, seemingly very embarrassed as he answered a very quiet 'That's why I'm here'.

Those words resonated through Aurora's head as she realized the full extent of what that simple sentence meant. Peregrith, her only trusted companion and guide didn't know anymore of this legend than she did! Clueless, absolutely clueless and as blind as she was… They were so screwed…

Gathering up some stability and as much poise as she could muster in herself, Aurora played her poker-face, something she was good at doing when her mother yelled at her for skipping classes. As still as stone, she glanced over at Peregrith who had the exact same expression on his face. She had to smile at that.

The old man sighed heavily, as though physically exhausted by the two's oblivious ignorance. He stood, grunted the reply of a typical old grump and went behind the counter, pulling out a rolled up piece of cloth. Lazily sitting back in his chair, Panther looked at Peregrith as he sipped from his pint of ale.

"Get the girl a drink, Boy! Think ye would know manners." He exclaimed coolly. Peregrith jumped out of his seat and lept across the room like he was a frightened little doe. The big bear of a man loomed at Aurora, giving her the impression that he was once a great warrior in his time. The man's presence demanded respect and obedience within the room; Aurora hadn't noticed that earlier that day, though it was hard to notice anything having had her face planted to the floorboards before then. He was dark skinned with jet black hair, braided beard and moustache with a big pair of deep grey eyes piercing your soul at a glance. He wasn't fat so much as well built and healthily fed, but the scars ranging across his jaw and hands gave away a tale of hardship and barbaric survival. He was one of those who had the capability to crush you into mush, but that you knew could never harm a bird; still, the possibility of his massive power sent chills running down Aurora's spine.

Panther rolled out the cloth on Aurora's lap and she quickly got hold of the edges as she scanned the odd scratches upon the textile. It was a continental map with the title '*Avalon*' written at the top. The thing began to give Aurora a headache the more she looked at it, eventually she couldn't help but look away.

"Don't turn your head, Girl. It hurts at first but look quick and memorizes the points on the map, their location, and the distance between each. God forbid if ye and Pery get separated, ye will have to continue without one another."

Aurora did as Panther said and scanned the map, every hill, every river, every valley that led to nowhere. The more she concentrated, the more she could see that parts of the map moved. The forest canopies swayed in the breeze and the grasslands rippled like waves in the wind. Streams flowed and the roads were occupied by travellers and beasts of burden. It was as though she were flying across the land, swiftly scanning the surrounding landscape. She could *feel* herself gliding their path through the sky, along the forest trails, drifting on a shallow glistening lake, stalking down a mountain pass.

The man snatched the map away, rolling it back up and

holding it protectively in his bear-like paws. He looked at her carefully as though waiting for her to freak out or throw up. Peregrith came back with a pint of ale mixed with cranberry juice and handed it to Aurora. He was taken aback at how pale and shaky she was. She took the glass happily and couldn't believe how weak she felt. Feeling parched she downed the entire glass in two big gulps and sighed in contentment, holding out the empty glass to Peregrith for seconds. Both gazed at her in astonishment for a moment before Peregrith went to get her another and Panther let out a light impressed whistle.

Silenced ensued once more. It was peaceful, relaxing and serene; until Aurora let out a massive beer belch that rattled the windows clear of their dust. The silence was broken with Peregrith's small fit of laughter as he came back with another full glass of fruilli in his hand.

"And you talk to me about manners…" Peregrith muttered between hiccups of laughter.

"… Shut up, Boy…" The man mumbled behind his hand which was holding a smirk out of sight. "-Besides you threw up when you first sighted that map…" Peregrith stifled his laugh and fell into complete seriousness as he looked into the dancing flames in front of them. "Did you manage to take a good look?"

Aurora nodded wordlessly, too embarrassed to speak. Panther grunted softly in acknowledgement and sighed sleepily. Without a word the man stood and left the serenity of the flames, leaving Aurora and her companion alone yet again.

The silence between them was as thick as butter. There were so many questions Aurora wanted to ask, but really had no idea where to start.

"I was to merry Liza many years ago." Peregrith stated in an almost inaudible whisper. Aurora glanced over, but he wouldn't meet her eyes. "She's Panthers daughter. He didn't mind me as far as I could tell, but he said no. Nearly broke her heart."

"-And what about yours?" She whispered gently, unsure if she wanted to delve there.

The pain that swam within his eyes seemed as a ghost from the past, unable to escape the prison of a mortal's heart. They shone dimly of time that has passed effortlessly in the face of this boy, this boy who seemed all too old to know of such things.

Aurora wanted to comfort him, this boy with an ancient all knowing soul, but she resisted temptation if only for saving herself from feeling the fool. Suddenly she felt exceedingly tired and slightly drunk as she rose from her chair to retire to bed. As she climbed the stairs she took one last look at her friend. Seeing the glimmer of a tear shine against the firelight, her stomach clenched and she regretted not saying something. Her pride refused to recede and she retreated back to the room where she could only hope for more courage for the upcoming journey.

Chapter
Nine

Aurora woke with a start, the fresh morning light cascading over her face as she turned to greet Peregrith who was once again no where to be found. Aurora rolled her eyes and got out of bed smooshing her face with her hands in hope of waking up.

Aurora nearly jumped out of her skin as Peregrith came rushing in, a look of sudden urgency plastered all over his face. He grabbed their bags, stuffed what was there into them and without saying a word flung Aurora's cloak at her, telling her to put it on.

"G'morning to you too…" She muttered complacently.

"No time to explain; Liza. Gotta get out before Liza comes!" He exclaimed harshly, throwing one of the bags at her as he pushed them both out the door.

And Liza was there, smack dab in front of their faces as both came to a hurtling stop. Still as wild and fiery looking as the night before, the woman stood in the hall, three drinks in hand and an eerie, suspicious, mischievous look about her. She smiled, and Aurora almost peed herself with how creepy the woman looked.

"-Have a drink before you go Pery… It'll warm your spirits." She said as temptingly as a creepy old woman could muster. Peregrith paused a moment, silence ensuing every audible heartbeat as he thought it over in his mind.

"No-thanks!" He exclaimed loudly as he grabbed Aurora's hand and fled down the stairs and out the little Inn. Both Aurora and Peregrith could hear the vicious sobs and loud babbling from the love-crazed woman as they rushed down the street, trying their hardest not to seem obvious to the locals. They raced around a corner and into a little general goods corner shop.

The clerk lifted his head wearily and gave a cunning grin.

"Out with yer woman der Pery?" The man slurred coolly.

Peregrith rolled his eyes dramatically and gave a little chuckle. "Strict business Dale…" The man chuckled in quiet disbelief as he pulled out a clean sheet of parchment and quill.

"What will it be, boy?"

Peregrith didn't reply at first as he loomed over the bits and bobs of little trinket magicry. Aurora wasn't interested enough to hear the drawling on of their grocery list, she was much more interested in the weapons and books they had in the far right corner.

The faint musty odour of old books drifted around Aurora as she scrolled through the titles of each little novella; everything from an 'Avalonian Guide' to 'The WitchHaze Cultists Journal' lined the three rows of texts. The more she scanned each book, the more one particular title seemed to beckon for her to remove it from the company of the others; 'Three Fates of Avalonia'. She caressed the spine and a sense of dread coursed through her veins. Quickly retracting her hand as though it had violently shocked her, she moved on to the weapons that sat perched upon the wall.

Swords, axes, bows, arrows, throwing stars and almost every other weapon one could think of was perched before her. All of which were made of silver and a soft cobalt-blue metal that seemed to glow the more you looked at it. Aurora picked up one of the daggers, almost dropping it from it being so light. The blade was thin, double edged and scrolled with rune-like symbols that glowed the same cobalt-blue that accented the handle.

"It's gorgeous isn't it?" A voice muttered into her ear, scaring her shitless and making her cut open her finger carelessly.

"What the hell Pery!" She exclaimed, clearly pissed more that he startled her than the blood that was now running down her sleeve. He took her finger and swiped his hand over it, making the cut seal and vanish without a trace. Aurora stood there bewildered with awe, unable to comprehend what her eyes just witnessed.

Peregrith handed her a small wand-shaped bundle wrapped in a dark green canvas and twine. "Don't open it until we're outside the town. People would kill to have what's in that." He muttered cautiously as he moved to step out of the shop.

"Don't go get culled now, Pery... Remember our bargain!" The man drawled as he turned his attention to the little pile of coin Pery had given him for his service. Only then did Aurora realize the sack of meat and fir was absent from Pery's back.

He strode out into the morning's rays with Aurora close on his heels. They may be better prepared now for the tremendous journey ahead of them, but it still didn't help that as much as Peregrith wanted to. He knew what they were going up against and made him break into a cold sweat just thinking about it.

Aurora and Pery slipped out of sight as the town occupant's daily lives continued as it had for eons. A family of farmers walked ahead of them just out of earshot. All seven of them sang and laughed, totally oblivious to anyone around them as they strolled home with two loaded bags on the old pack-mule that seemed as happy as they did. Aurora couldn't help but smile; it warmed her heart how much family could effect the happiness of ones life.

They turned left at the next fork as Aurora and Pery took the right. Before very long, the laughter and happiness of that little family faded to a peaceful silence.

"-So what do you owe the shopkeeper?" Aurora asked slyly, glancing behind them to make sure they were definitely alone.

"Open the package." He stated quietly.

Aurora took the package from her bag and slowly unwrapped it, curious as to why it was wrapped so delicately. Carefully undoing the binding and unfolding the cloth, Aurora gazed upon a thin, oddly shaped dagger no thicker than her finger and as dainty as a new-born kitten. It was the same kind of weapon at that shop; silver body with edges of cobalt-blue. It gleamed in the sunlight, as though it was its own source of energy, as bright as the sun.

"This is what I owe the man for..." Pery muttered prideful. "-It's a weapon that never gets dull, meant to hide away up a sleeve or ankle. Worth it's weight in gold too, I assure you."

"And you could afforded one? Surely that skin and meat wasn't worth that much?" Aurora exclaimed in deep awe.

"That's between me and Dale." He stated darkly, his face hiding yet another secret. A chill ran down her spine as she kept pace with him, almost certain that the blade would demand blood or worse yet, souls. "Now keep it wrapped up in the cloth, Milady. If someone was to seen such a treasure, we would be knee deep in a fight quicker than you could say *trouble...*"

Aurora nodded and carefully wrapped it back up, taking particular care not to nick herself while doing so.

"How does it not cut through?"

"The suade comes with each blade and can be fashioned into a sheath, given the time and skill to do so. " Pery muttered quietly, only half attentive as he stared out into the woods and slowed to a stop. Aurora froze in place and scanned the surrounding bush, trying to identify what Pery saw. Movement caught her gaze, for just a split second and she could feel the breath leave her chest. A large clump of fur and paws strolled through the forest not a hundred feet away. Its massive jaws clamped open and shut as grunts and little growls escaped from behind pointed teeth. The bear was as big as Aurora had imagined one would be, but it still caught her off guard to be so close to one.

Ignoring the two travellers completely, the large brown ball of hair tottered out of sight and Pery instantly fell at ease. Aurora, forgetting to breath, fell directly to the dirt beneath her in a cold sweaty faint.

Peregrith, not even remotely phased, took her by the waist and hoisted her up in one foul swoop; steadying her while she regained her balance and brains. Pery just grinned, patted her shoulder mockingly, and continued down the road at a complaisant gate.

A loud roar echoed through the woods a quarter mile back, birds fleeing from the violence. Deep Yells of angry devils resounded through the trees, mingling with the terrified cries of the massive beast. Aslaiks had caught up to the bear, and unfortunately would soon catch up to them. Pery groaned at the cognizance that there would be no relaxing stroll today, not while those things were around.

They cut through the forest, neglecting to follow any trail crafted by man or animal. They would have to take care with a herd of aslaiks on their ass. Pery still couldn't tell if it was mere coincidence that the beasts were everywhere, or if they actually knew that the Princess had returned to their world. It chilled him to think of them finding her in the middle of the night, him asleep and Aurora defenceless against them. Would she know to run if it came to it? Would she fight back? Could she? He soon decided that a little hidden blade, in the wake of what would be laid before them, might not be enough to save her life.

The wind blew forcefully against the poplars, making it hard for Pery to concentrate on where he was going. Through all his years of living on the peninsula, he had never ventured further than that little town on his own. When his parents still lived, they had taken him to it by horseback, but he was no more than a babe then and it would not help him now.

"North... Must follow north." He mumbled to himself under his breath. Aurora glanced at him curiously, but said nothing. Pery chanced a glance at her and noticed how pale and sweaty she had become. At first he thought it was just because she was tired, but the more time pressed on, the further behind she would fall and the heavier her breathing became. Abruptly turning and facing her he gently forced her down onto a log, without saying a word. As much as Aurora wanted to ask, she didn't care enough to even blink.

"Look at me, Aurora." He said sternly, startling Aurora enough to listen. The amount of authority he could implant in his voice sent a chilling sensation down her spine and to her gut. Her eyes fell onto his and were glassy, distant and non-responsive. In his mind he began to panic; he knew exactly what was wrong, had seen it thousands of times before from local villages.

The families of the sick would come to Kanna in search of medicine, those of which were sick as well, in the first stages before they were unable to walk. The sickness moved fast through the people. Within hours entire villages would become desolate and lifeless, the sickness sweeping the land like a plague. He didn't expect for Aurora to catch sickness so quickly- especially knowing what blood ran through her veins.

Pery quickly wrapped Aurora's arm around his shoulder as he hurried her through the now darkening forest. Twilight threatened with death as they pushed forward, terrified that they would be caught off guard and vulnerable. His mind blurred as everything began melting into itself; the trees all looked the same, there was no light for direction and the far-off calling of wolves vibrated through his head.

The melancholy music of the night echoed through the woods and wrapped itself around them; threatening, toying and whispering their panic to one another. Aurora began to fall out of consciousness, holding on only by the small pleadings of her friend's voice. Reality began to slip with every stumbling stride she took and she couldn't help but feel alone next to the strong body that hauled her around like a group of oxen. The howls and movements of creatures drew nearer as the crescent moon peaked through the canopy of leaves overhead, obscured momentarily by cotton-shaped clouds that drifted swiftly past the dainty splinter.

Eyes glowed in the night, all around them, pressing them into a sense of fearful abandon. Growls and silent whines bounced off the trees as Pery's heart raced to the rhythm of his thoughts.

Within a moment the forest became still, and nothing but the slow trickling of a nearby stream could be heard in the dense woods. The eyes drew back; the owls and birds stopped their questions. Then the rambling chatter of beastly-creatures caught his ear. It was too dark to see, and the group of aslaiks sounded like they were coming from every direction. Pery caught his breath, snapped from his frozen stance and sped down to the sound of the trickling water.

Fireflies danced around them as Pery hauled Aurora through the shallow indent the once glorious brook had made. The stones which lay sleeping beneath their feet, moved and groaned as the two human's body weight was placed upon them. Pery slipped upon the salty slime and went face first into the sandy earth on the other side. Hearing the aslaik herd just behind them, he took firm hold of Aurora, who was now mostly unconscious, and fled to the security and shelter of a large jagged stone to which the creek made birth.

Pery's eyes adjusted to the night, just in time to duck from view of one of the beasts. His heart lifted as a gap in the rock came into view, wide enough to fit a person through. Pulling Aurora by the shoulders, he dragged her into the small hollowed cave and waited silently for the aslaiks to pass. As soon as the course rasps of the beasts faded from earshot, he made for the forest.

"-Pery … Don't leave- me…." Came a weak, barely audible voice from the centre of the cavern. Pery shot his head at Aurora's direction and realized she had regained consciousness, if only for a brief moment. He slowly went back to her, cupped her face in his hands and felt her burning flesh upon his rough palms. She was fading and fast; He couldn't wait any longer, if he didn't find it now, he would be too late.

"Milady… Aurora, listen to me carefully." He spoke calm but clearly, "Do not die on me, alright! You will get better just don't fall asleep…" He whispered with trembling lips. It was the second time in his life he had said that, and the previous experience ended in horror. He bolted through the opening of the cave and back into the darkness of the night, hoping upon hope that he wouldn't come back too late.

⬕————————————➤

Unconsciousness took her into a world she would much rather not be; her own personal hell of spitting fires and never ending secrets, lies, and death. Every corner she turned was a new giezer of wicked truths and unwanted realizations of a mortal life. In every direction Aurora witnessed the pain and gruesome tortures her people had suffered in her absence. Images of her mother and grandmother came to light like an aging reel of history.

Her grandmother stood before the crowds of her people and demanded blood in place of safety. War broke loose and a seemingly familiar masked woman faced up against her. Both fought brutally and with little honour, like that of siblings squabbling over candy. Blood painted the scene and the image of Aurora's grandmother's victory warped into something of darkness and dread.

It was Aurora's mother that appeared before her now. Young and as beautiful as heaven, the woman's smile shone through all others in the crowd. Her happiness was measured in smiles as a child appeared from behind the blissful garden gate. The child was like a cherub, plump and giddy from the dose of wonder her mother always gave forth, and the wings that fluttered from her shoulder-blades that caught notice to all others in the garden. All gasped in shock as the child's father emerged from the shadows of the towering wall, unwilling or unable to enter.

It was the man's face that stuck in her mind, a face that could not be seen, but was almost felt upon her memory. Aurora could feel her inner self gasping for air as she tried to unravel that little secret, that face that her mind tried so desperately hard to forget. In another instant, Aurora's mother and the child was dragged away behind castle walls as the Grandmother wordlessly screamed at the man, banishing him from Avalon.

Pain surged through Aurora's mind as she tried to grasp firmly onto what she witnessed next. Her vision became bloodied and fuzzy as she watched with horror, the child's wings being sliced from her body and the marks left by them being burned to stop the bleeding. The child wailed and screamed in pain as Aurora's mother cried and fought against the guards' hold. The grandmother turned her back to the child and beckoned the guards to take the child away. It lay there weeping, in shock from the pain, looking like no more than a normal child off the streets; her glow was gone, face flush yet pale, hair raggedy from the blood that tangled it's golden curl, and an emptiness in her chocolate eyes that made her no better than the rest.

"Aurora… Aurora?" a familiar voice rang within her throbbing head. "Princess, it's time to wake…" Aurora opened her eyes and gazed into the face of a very dirty young boy.

"… Pery?" She mumbled coarsely as she tried to sit up and failed, almost barfing onto her sticky face. Raising her hand weakly to her mouth, she touched her fingertips to her lips and tried focusing her gaze upon what had coated her fingers so readily. It was red and had the scent of copper. She was covered in blood.

"… What -the hell?" She mumbled weakly, almost passing out from the scent of it. Pery shook his head and offered her up some naucious smelling brewed tea. Aurora took it, glanced at the flowers and various roots that still floated in it, held her nose and chugged half of it down, throwing most of it up again as the taste hit her tongue. Bracing herself for the second swig, she managed to keep it down, with only a minor funny face to exhibit.

After the vile liquid was gone, she gazed around the dark and damp hole they were crammed into and nearly jumped out of her skin as she stared face to face with the ugliest god-forsaken creature that could ever have walked the planet. Worst of it all, was that there were five of them; huge, smelly, beastly creatures that looked as though they were about to kill you even though they were already dead.

"What in the Holy-Mother-Of-God are those!" She hyperventilated, nearing hysteria the longer she looked at them.

Pery glanced at them as if they were nothing and shrugged it off as he moved to sit lazily beside Aurora.

"Pery…" She asked as sternly as she could muster as she motioned to the heap of bodies a couple feet away from them, "What the hell?" Was all she could get out of her gaping mouth.

"-When I found the place three days ago, they were around here searching for us. I couldn't let them find us, so I killed them…"

A little light went on in Aurora's head, "… Three days… ago?" She whispered softly to herself, fingers twitching a bit. *'What the hell…'* She thought to herself.

"I couldn't let them be found by other Aslaiks, so I dragged them all in here." He said proudly, more to himself than her.

Aurora just stared at him, then at the bodies, and found herself wanting to freak out on the whole situation. Taking a deep breath she decided to stay silent. After all, a large pile of dead bodies wasn't the end of the world, just wretchedly disgusting.

"-So… Three days?" She managed to mutter out of her clamped shut jaw. "What was wrong with me?"

"… Caught The Silent Death. You're lucky I found the right plant around here… not exactly a common weed."

"-But I still feel so sick."

"It's the side effects of the plant; puts your body into overdrive and make you feel very weak. You'll be as right as rain tomorrow…"

Aurora looked at the smelly bodies a few feet from her, moaned and curled up on a ball under her cloak. Within moments she was back asleep with Pery curled up beside her. *Three days of hell, and they were still surprisingly alive…* Pery took one last glance at the dead bodies and Aurora's still blood soaked cloths… *Hazah for them.*

When dawn broke over the tree-line and cascaded into the little cave, Aurora rose, feeling refreshed and stiff. The day looked promising as she peeked her head out of the cavern's mouth. Birds sang illustriously and expressed their joys vicariously through their tunes. Carefully creeping to the nearby stream to rinse away the blood and weakness that still gripped her, she noticed with glee that she wasn't as bad as the day before. Aurora smiled and with the image of serenity in her mind went back inside to get ready to leave. That feeling of serenity was slashed however, when the sight of Pery ruffling through the dead beastly corpses made her almost gag.

"-What're you doing…?"She asked in total disgust.

"Looking for something useful." He stated as if to a child, "They don't carry money with them, but a lot of times they keep shiny things like jewels and weapons- it depends on if the group is new to the game or not… and by the looks of this group, I would assume they are." He said pointing towards the little pile of hand-made tools that looked as though they were crafted from bones and stones.

"This however, "He stated triumphantly, as he held up a rusted old sword, no longer than arms length and handed it to Aurora. "Will work perfectly for now."

Aurora took firm hold of the weapon, gazing at its experienced majestic beauty, sheath semi-dangling from the shaft of the blade. The steel felt good in her grasp, and yet her hesitance came from not having a clue how to wield it. She scanned it from tip to tip and glanced at Pery helplessly.

"I'll give you pointers later." He said delicately. Aurora nodded and looped it onto her belt before she grabbed her bag, which felt half a pound lighter. Suspicion wanted to fill her mind, but she refused to let it get in her way. Swallowing her questions, she let them simmer in her gullet as they left the security of the little cavern.

The sunlight was blinding, yet so warm to her skin, which had turned a pale peach in its absence; it instilled a hopefulness that few things in the world ever had for her. The life of the forest and everything that moved in it, the rippling of the stream and the birds that took to the sky, everything was hers to help protect, and whether she liked it or not, they were indeed *hers*. It instilled a sense of pride to such ownership, such honour to be part of such a miraculous and magical world, even with the dark parts that go with it. As they pressed on through the dancing trees, she knew that they had hope; just as long as the rest of Avalonia did, they both had hope to come out alive.

Chapter Ten

The day dragged on for hours without any occurrences. Aurora and Pery stuck to the main road north through the forest that was densely populated with golden maple. They crossed no one's path and the world seemed as empty and silent as the dead.

The only sounds that accompanied them were those of the birds that seemed to follow their every step. It was cute at first, but after an hour the actions seemed purposeful and threatening. Aurora gazed inconspicuously around her, watching and waiting for the little balls of feathers to dart their attacks, but they remained aloof and perched comfortably at a distance.

"They won't bother you." Pery muttered in a half-mumble. Aurora looked at him uncomfortably but kept her worries to herself. "They're Isietha's eyes… trained spies of the skies."

Aurora shot him an inquisitive look, waiting for the explanation that was almost demanded by the comment. He glanced unwillingly at her and took a big breath to steady his thoughts. Pery always found that with telling the truth on any matter there were always two reactions that could take place. One, is that it would be accepted gracefully and without question. The other, a hurricane of accusational and messy emotions would ensue. As much as Pery hated taking the chance of having to endure the hurricane, he hated keeping the truth from those he was allied with.

"I worked with Isietha a couple hundred years ago." Is what slipped out of his mouth, expression effortlessly cool and collected. "When the Queen, your Grandmother, reined over Avalonia, Isietha held charge over the knights and the protection of the realm. At the time, Isietha wasn't the evil she is known to be today; during the Northern Wars."

Pery fell silent and couldn't look at Aurora, but she waited patiently, silently giving him the courage she knew he didn't have to tell anyone else.

"-I killed a lot of people during that time..." He whispered painfully, "and I thought it was for the good of everything, but after words; after the blood and lives lay upon my hands I knew that what I had done was wrong. You have no idea how much it hurts to tell you of all people, this scar upon my past. Someone who has only known me for the better part of a fortnight... I feel as though I've known you my whole life."

The sun caressed his cold form as Aurora gently touched his shaking shoulder, his face turned away in shame and sadness. Pery didn't want her to see the tears that rolled down his cheeks. Her touch seemed to shrink him further into the sadness that engulfed his soul. He clutched his arms around himself, as if trying to hold his broken-soul together, silently asking the Gods for understanding.

"I am your friend Pery, as you are mine, and like you said-we've only known each other for days and it does seem longer... But I assure you that whatever you've done in the past will not condemn my trust in you. I trust you, Peregrith, with every grain of my existence. I trust that you know what's right from wrong." She stated as gently as she could, without trying to sound awkward. She then confidently grabbed his arm and pulled him from the shadows of his memories; back into the shaky confines of reality. "Since I have no one else in this world who will help me, you are my pillar and my stone... Don't let me crumble; don't let me fall."

Pery stared at her and took in a deep breath, immortalizing

those words inside himself before he gave a sharp nod and placed his rough hand firm upon hers. He had to smile at himself at the thought of having an actual friend all to himself. All his life he never had anyone that he could trust any of his secrets to; not even Kanna, who so lovingly took him into her home. If Pery was her pillar and stone, Aurora was his light in the darkness of this world. Could he trust her with that darkness though; would she stand firmly beside her friend, or would she flee like Isietha so boldly said she would so many years back?

The wind wrapped around the grove as it ran through the trees, twirling and elegantly flying with them as they trotted down the trail. Every hour that passed, the scenery remained the same; trees, underbrush and the various wildlife that scurried about, to which were blissfully oblivious to them, remained unchanged and still very wild. It wasn't until the slight scent of salty air hitting Aurora's nostrils that she began to pay attention to her surroundings again.

It blew her thoughts right out of the clouds and into her own world again. The exhaustion that came from a full day's walk eroded away as they caught sight of the most beautiful sunset either had ever witnessed before in their lives. The orange rays caught the gentle rippling gleams of the lake and made the water glow in an iridescent milky blue. Waves lapsed over silky golden sand not ten yards away, washing in the sounds and smells of a shining tropical oasis. A ring of evergreens lined the shoreline, tilting ever so slightly towards the water, as if taking in the majestic smell of the ocean blue. Seagulls glided overhead, calling and crying to their fellow birds to which they would compete for the biggest and juiciest insect lining the top of the lake. Aurora couldn't believe her eyes, and she couldn't help but want more.

Rapidly ripping her shoes and socks from her feet, Aurora didn't hesitate to feel that golden sand squish between her aching toes. Pery smiled and followed suit, both wading a couple of feet into the clear depths of the water's edge.

"-This was almost worth the insane walk here." Aurora

muttered more to herself than her companion. Pery nodded in silent agreement as they walked side by side along the beach, feet coated in a luscious liquid that seemed to rejuvenate them almost instantly.

Aurora turned over the situation in her head and couldn't help but ask aloud, "Why is the water salty and… well, magical?"

"A unicorn and her bane have walked these shores for ages… and the lake is fed by multiple rivers that come in from the Lapidus Ocean to the west of us. It's what gives this place its unique allurement. They call it *Ezers Brinums* or *The Lake of Wonders;* People used to come from all over Avalon to be healed here…"

Aurora looked around in search of another living soul, yet there was none to be found. She could envision families and travellers, lovers and old men wading into the salty depths. Memories; they are no more than buried memories of ancient souls. There was a mystery to those waters that she could feel were hidden deep in her bones. Ancient words of sprites and ghosts crawled through the thickness of the evening air, wafting upon them like the waves that lapped over their feet. Aurora snuck a look at Pery to see if he could hear them too. His face held an expression she had never seen on him before; peace, he looked at peace with the world. Pery's smile crossed his shining face as he stared into a world Aurora could not see. She didn't question it; just let it flow as they strolled blissfully along the water's edge.

←————————→

They camped out near the lake's shore, sounds of water lapping over the fine-grained sand reaching their make-shift camp. Aurora watched the campfire flames dance in what was left of the evening's light. Owls and frogs filled the air with their songs, lulling Aurora into a peaceful state of contentment. Pery, however, remained rigid and cautiously wary of their surroundings. Something didn't feel right to him and made him uneasy towards the encroaching night.

"I'm gonna check out the area." Pery said sternly as he quickly got to his feet and walked into the woods without another word. Aurora was left by the fire, confused and suddenly alone, staring into the darkness after her friend.

The night remained deafeningly alive with the nocturnal beasts that roamed amidst the trees. Little mammals, birds and all manners of slithery and slimy creatures freely walked in the open around the warmth of the fire, far enough away to show only silhouettes, yet close enough to give away their obvious curiosity. She had to laugh at the creatures natural instincts to fear all forms of predators, and yet so defiantly break those instincts because of simple curiosity. She couldn't tell if that made them exceptionally fool-hearty, or exceptionally brave.

A faint whisper of a sound made its way through the trees, hovering above Aurora as she cocked her head to listen. She could tell instantly that the noise was that of a struggling animal, and not a small one at that. Her gut clenched as she silently stood and began creeping towards the sound.

The fire's comforting glow faded as she made her way deeper into the trees towards the phantom sound. Gently, Aurora slid her little dagger from its cloth scabbard and got ready to strike. If the creature was going to attack her, she refused to go down without a fight.

Stifling the urge to gasp, she froze at the sight her eyes were now witnessing. A grey roan mare lay amidst moss bedding with a pure black new-born foal at her feet. Even more remarkable was the matching pair of horns extruding from both animals' foreheads. The horn curved and twisted with an arcane glowing essence that beckoned any stranger forth to their destruction.

'It has been foretold of your coming, young daughter.'

Aurora blinked from her trance. Had the horse just spoken to her?

'The birth of my Bane is the omen of change. Your spirit, young goddess, is what strains my soul.' The mother Unicorn

whispered into Aurora's mind. The creature was too unearthly beautiful to gaze upon and Aurora had to turn away. She knew all too well what change the mother was speaking of.

The mother's voice echoed wisdom and ancient knowledge that reminded Aurora of Kanna and by-the-by, her deceased Grandmother whom always had something to say to her granddaughter.

"Why am I here Mother…" Aurora muttering, barely audible in the calling of the night. "Why me…" All the hidden fear and strain began rippling through her as she sank to her knees and bowed her head in silent defeat, tears escaping the confines of their prison.

'Your spirit has called you here, daughter.' The voice spoke softly, *'Your inner self knows and you refuse to listen. You have become spoiled and tainted from the other-world and refuse to accept the change that must happen to everyone. Death is not the end for any living thing and most cannot choose when they cross to this world, yet you can. Daughter I implore you to stand aside from your cowardly self and take up the journey of which your spirit is calling for. You are beyond mortal young one, and must realize you are here because of that.'*

A chill of understanding swept through her then as she rose with a better discerning of her path; this conquest of the elements that would some how sooth her agitated spirit. Faint echoes of a familiar voice caught Aurora's attention then as she whirled to the direction of their campfire; Pery was calling for her.

She had so many questions left unanswered she was ready to spew at the mother unicorn, but when she turned back, the beast and her bane were gone. A sense of dread crossed her features as she frantically searched the lilac grove that encased the creatures. Dread became defeat as she gave up her endeavours and turned towards the source of Pery's calls.

'Patience, daughter; You have your entire life to discover answers to your curiosity… and when you have found the answers to

why you have come and still wish to return to the other realm, my Bane
will emerge upon the path home.'

With those last words, Aurora felt herself truly apart from the presence of the realms mystic wonders.

Aurora appeared from the encompassing trees that surrounded the campfire; still holding her dagger defensively, eyes a million miles from there. Pery was shocked silent and slowly crept towards the far-off maiden, taking care not to move too quickly, and took the dagger from her loose grip. Glancing powerfully into his eyes, she seemed to gore out his worry as she let out a massive sigh and collapsed heavily beside the fire, diligently wrapping the warmth of the woollen blanket around her chilled frame.

He watched as Aurora slept peacefully, though shivering from the night's chill. The season's frost was fast approaching and he threw another log on the fire. Knowing they would have to find better clothing for the snowy months, Pery cringed at the thought of the next town. It was a holy village a couple of leagues north, hidden amidst the trees, past the river. Last time he was there was during the great wars, when the village had been burned to the ground. Uneasiness ran through him as he fell into a disturbed sleep, thoughts still wrapped around what Aurora had discovered from the lake spirits as they played their otherworldly games and tricks.

Chapter Eleven

She was gone for hours in the dark... Did she follow a sprite? Try to look for me? I'm putting her in more danger by not showing her the powers of this world, but I don't want to scare her off! She will learn her bloodline's power on her own, but barely knows how to shield herself right now, let alone how to strike back. This world will either tear her asunder or build that girl up to a new height unlike which she's ever experienced. She needs time though, time of which is fading faster than neither of us would be able to grasp on to. Oh how I wish she were the old crone that was prophesized, with some real wisdom about her... if only she knew her own legend...

Pery watched his friend as she stirred from her restless sleep, breath caught in the chill of the early morning light. Her eyes found Pery's still figure standing against a tall oak tree.

"Good morn." He muttered with a forced grin. Aurora grunted her reply as she uncurled herself and clamoured groggily to the lake shore. Splashing the icy cold water across her face, Aurora felt better than she had for days... colder, yet better. Even Aurora noticed how chilly the nights, and in turn, early mornings were beginning to be. She had to laugh at herself as she realized that it took a mystically mythic creature to tell her to smarten up, before she did so herself. After all, when everything was said and done, Aurora would get to go home when the world was saved.

Breakfast was spent quietly contemplating the village to come. Pery explained to his companion that the village, though abandoned and mostly in ruins, still is home to ghosts and dark things. Most people keep far from it though and therefore, most trouble won't come from anything that's living. She wasn't worried too much about solid creatures; it's those that drift through walls that scared her senseless.

They spent hours slowly trodding through the forest, abandoning the security of the trails for the speed of the road. Aurora tried with little success to hide her boredom as sigh after sigh escaped her; she never would have thought in a million years that such an amazing journey would be so painfully tedious.

The rippling of a nearby creek reached Aurora's ears as her pace began to escalate to a near run, Pery gazing bewilderingly at her enthusiasm for mere water as he silently trailed after her. Aurora's flesh shivered as she approached the creek, an eerily familiar sound vibrating through the air before her. As the creek came into view, something in the corner of her eye made her stop. By the time she turned her head the creature was gone, as was the song it was singing. Goosebumps covered her skin as Pery silently loped beside her.

With a questioning look from her comrade, Aurora kept her mouth shut as she tried inconspicuously to clear her throat.

"-Huh…" Pery muttered more to himself as he relaxed his stance and stared at his companion, as though studying her odd movements for early signs of insanity.

"-I, uh… thought I heard…"

Realization hit Pery square in the face as Aurora mumbled quietly to him what exactly she saw. Sprites, water sprites to be exact, is what drew her: little mischievous forest spirits that were well known to lure young children into the water in a trance-like state, so they might consume their soul. A chill ran down Aurora's spine at the thought of children drowning; It's as bad as throwing a kitten into a deep lake.

With a bit more wariness, the two made their way back onto the road and soon found themselves upon the gates of an old abandoned village tucked away inside the jumble of trees that was the ancient forest surrounding them. The light filtered through the golden canopy overhead, producing a very misty and eerie scene that made Aurora's stomach knot with caution. Piles of rubble, stone and old mortar lie between buildings that were in serious disrepair. Every step they took brought them further into a creepy nightmare of dark shadows, crows and a cold wind that stole the warmth right from your bones. Old crusty blood painted some of the buildings from years long gone, giving colour to the lurid grey necropolis. Low, hollow groans came from the darkness in each standing building. Without a doubt, the place was definitely haunted.

The two lurked into the first building that didn't look like it would implode upon itself . It was a temple complete with solid white pillars, large fire scones, dried lifeless flowers and a large stagnant pool of water with a flat altar placed in the centre. The scones were unlit, by the look of the dust layering every crevice they have been unused for an eon at the least.

An omniscient, dark, godlike presence clung upon their shoulders, pinning them in place before the elegant carving strewn into the native rock. It was calm in the temple, shadows mocking their growing fears, and all that lit their path was the small hole in the roof that leaked green light from the world above. The carving depicted a city of stone and fire. Three warrior goddesses that held fast to three nearly identical weapons of death. All three of the women were fierce in their passion for blood, all of which stood over a pile of bloodied carcasses. The one laughing maniacally as her opponent's severed head rolled to her sisters feet. Another showed a crazed euphoria astride a gored demon. While the last cupped her hands in offering to the moon that shone brilliantly behind them. All three of them had the life essence of their victims stained to their skin, their long teeth gleaming with their pleasure. They were destruction; death; the maidens of darkness. All these things, yet only one word rang through Aurora's mind… Vampire.

Aurora clung to Pery's arm in shock as it all clicked in to place. The villagers had worshipped these demons. Suddenly the red stone altar in the centre of the pool seemed to crawl with the blood of the innocent. Spirits seemed to be awakened by their mere presence. The air began to feel cold, and the shadows suddenly felt more surreal than castoffs of light.

Pery steadied his comrade, silently assuring her of the absence of any real danger. Ghosts were just ghosts after all. Each breath became more laboured as the tension in the chamber heightened. The silence in the building was squeezing the very life from their bodies as they stood before the mural paralyzed by the unknown. The silence was deafening.

"CAWH!"

The two darted to the wall, Pery pushing the girl behind him with sword drawn and ready.

"CAWH!"

They looked up and within the dimly lit temple, discovered the source of their terror. A crow sat perched within a large crack in the wall, glaring at them from behind great big orange eyes. Their panic levied slowly as the echos of random birds settled into the background. Both breathed a sigh of relief as Pery began to explore the dark arid temple. Aurora couldn't take her eyes off the bird; her mind kept inexplicably telling her to watch out.

"GRAAWH!" The creature bellowed from it's perch.

"Pery…" She whispered shakily, "-I think we should-"

Thousands of cries bellowed through the room, high pitched screeches vibrating off the smooth temple walls and bombarding the intruder's senses. Birds began erupting from every orifice, swooping and darting for the invaders as they tried pushing the humans from their sanctuary. A crumpled opening along the far wall promised an escape as they ducked and dodged their way across the pool.

The opening lead directly into a tunnel that twisted and turned in every direction imaginable. All the doors and archways that lead away were either locked shut or barred from the inside. Interwoven branches and thorns that were overgrown through the trellised tunnel became ample perches for the winged beasts in pursuit. Vines made of shadowed light seemed to be reaching out to entrap the humans who dared disrupt the wild grove as they darted passed. Time seemed unconsequential as they ran on through the system of paths that never seemed to part way. Yet after what seemed like hours of aimless running to nowhere, the overgrown pathway widened and funnelled them into the unknown realm that darkness always put forth.

The birds fell back from their prey as the two ran through the mouth of an underground cavern; made hollow and dark by the ancient rivers that used to flow through that region. The dark legion wrapped itself around the walls of the cavern, narrowly missing the two as the hoard flew passed. Aurora stumbled through the darkness in search of stability when her hand slipped upon the slick and slimy algae sleeping upon the cave's smooth surface. Their eye sight began adjusting to the near darkness, but still left them blind to the things they heard scurrying beneath their feet.

"Can we use that eye sight thingy again, Pery?" Aurora whined, her voice echoing across the vast empty space; making her sound ghost-like and surreal.

Pery shook his head and pointed towards the giant gap of light that peered through the dark at the far end of the cavern. "-Take hold of my arm and I'll guide you. I can't undo it on you if the spell is cast and you will be blinded where there is light…"

Aurora did what she was bid and clamped her grasp around his arm. Winding through the stalagmites that rose from the ground and narrowly missing their partners that hung above them, they made their way to the far off source of light. As they approached the growing light, both could make out the definition of a dark pool with a misty umbrella of water showering all around it from the spring in the centre. Aurora took a step back as the light broke apart and began drifting towards them; they were glowing orbs.

The splendid little balls of light floated down from their ceiling perch, illuminating the pool before them. Droplets of spring water crept down the stalactites, falling melodiously within the pool of water and ringing their song out into the chamber around them. By the glow of the dainty firebugs, she listened to the rhythm soothingly until the abnormal rhythm made her look deeper within its source. To Aurora's utter bewilderment, the drops were falling backwards; up into the ceiling from which it should have originated.

Pery silently placed his hand upon her shoulder, motioning to the bird that was slowly approaching the pool. They watched the winged beast drink of the deep waters, crooning softly to itself as it sat upon the ledge in anticipation. The creature was feeble and blind by the look of it's brilliantly clouded eyes, labouring to swallow the liquid now in it's beak. Moments later the bird snapped it's sightless gaze to the two intruders in his cavern, making clucking sounds of pain as it sunk to it's feet, letting out a terrifying shriek of death by it's last breath.

It sunk in very swiftly at the realization of what had just occurred and it sent a deep shiver down Aurora's spine. Words refused to escape her as she looked up at Pery in anguishing understanding. The boy just nodded his head in grievance and gently reeled her to an exit from the Hall of Death. The only sound that could be heard was the beating thume of wings in the darkness and their own shuffling foot falls. It seemed forbidden to speak of what they had just witnessed, that within that darkness lay a predator that would discover their presence by their voice; forbidden and wrong.

Just as they thought the darkness would never be cut by the rays of light, they emerged from the cavern into the blinding light of a mountain side opening. Fresh air hit them in one large gust and Aurora nearly collapsed by the release of that evil place's grasping confines.

They were miles from the village in an outcropping of a small mountainous hill overlooking miles and miles of wilderness towards the sinking sun. Beneath their feet was a full fifty-foot drop with short bushy trees trying to thrive in the rocky soil. It was scrub-land at it's finest and Aurora couldn't help but think that there might be a rattle snake or two between there and their next destination.

Small groves of bushes and abnormally tall grass awaited them at the base of the mountain as they picked their path through the loose stones. Every living plant was either a deep yellow, pale red, or a soft minty toothpaste-green, leaving the only thing to strike anyone's eyes being the bright crystalline white stones marbled with a bright turquoise blue; striking and slightly overwhelming to the senses.

The calls and melodies of surrounding wildlife remained steadfast in its familiarity. They sang and talked amidst themselves of the encroaching end to a lovely full day. The rustling of ground squirrels and invisible animals that couldn't be detected by the naked human eye reassured the two of little danger in their wake. For the first time in nearly that entire day they were nearly at ease.

A chill racked through them both as the wind picked up and the sun slowly started its decent over the horizon. The roughly hewn path became a stone-laid trail that they made their way along diagonally to the horizon, aiming to reach a thatch grove big enough to shelter them for the night. Their feet ached of weariness as they trudged on, almost missing the approach hidden in plain sight. A post sat perched at the fork with a poorly carved figure pointing to the right. Where ever the path led to was obstructed by a massive rough boulder that covered most of the road.

"Quietly My Lady – I am going to scout before us. Take heed to my warning and stay under cover." Pery muttered calmly as he slunk around the massive rock. He was shocked to hear his companion shuffle quietly not six inches behind him.

"… How about you go in front of me." She began as she carefully pulled out her blue dagger from its hidden sheath strapped to her thigh. "-and I will be careful to not cut you if something is about to pounce?" Pery's brow raised an inch at the thought of her actually attacking something and not nicking herself at the same time, and once the blood was produced, it would not stop. Such is the problem with magical blades, and not knowing quite how to wield them yet. There wasn't time for a lesson and the sound of arguing alone might cause unwanted company. Instead he withdrew a small blade from his ankle and presented it handle first.

"- You aren't ready to kill yet, Heiress, not with that. Leave the culling to an experienced hunter if the need arises…" Aurora began refusing with a look if impunity, but at the sight of Pery's pleading gaze, she thought it wiser to comply. "… Ok – stay close." He muttered as they strode passed the rock into completely unknown territory.

The sunset glowed across the hills, filtering through the brush and casting dark shadows in its wake. The treacherous climb down and up the path was more than Pery had expected as the path wound its way along the narrow ravines that ran parallel to the mountain base. Mosquito hawks swarmed around the two as they clung firmly onto the nearly vertical path. The sun was almost completely set when they took the last painstaking step up those impossible hills and were a hundred yards from a miniature cottage nestled tightly in the crevice of two large rock formations jutting from the earth at a 90 degree angle, one at its back and one at it's side. The same sort of bushy trees shielded the hut from sight; the only thing that could be seen was the wooden door that was intercepted by the stone-lain path.

Pery made a move to investigate the cottage, signalling Aurora to hold back until it was secured. He swiftly approached the door that stood an inch ajar and peeked inside. There was no fire in the hearth, no warmth to speak of, and a thick layer of grime marked nearly everything for its own. Drawing his sword, Pery slowly entered the one room hut, cringing inwardly as a loud pained creaking echoed through the small space. A large hole became evident in the farthest corner between the two rocks where it had been patched by poorly woven thatch. The lonely window in the hut, facing northeast towards the path, was the only aperture besides that of the door to let any form of light in, and it was barred by a barrel upon a half tilted table.

"… It's shelter, I suppose." Aurora muttered uneasily as she passed Pery through the door way and strolled into the abandoned hut. Her companion grunted his agreement as he lowered his sword, shrugging off the pack on his back while he was at it. Aurora's stomach turned and growled painfully at the thought of a good hot meal; hoping they could simply eat and sleep their aches away for the few hours they could. Seeing such a low supply of rations sent her into a frenzy of guilt that replaced her exhaustion with fretful insomnia.

The night fell into play outside the petite stone cottage. Owls called, frogs croaked, crickets chirped… it was almost peaceful in light of their soon to be predicament. They could only hope of finding some source of food in the morning to tide them over. Pery's eyes faltered and eventually closed with Aurora's getting heavier by the minute. It was definitely passed the witching hour by the time Aurora could convince herself that it was safe to rest, and with the last wisp of determination gone, fell into a deep sleep that an earth quake wouldn't be able to breach.

◆————————————————►

Aurora heard the door open first. Her breath caught in her throat as a silhouette of some gagly creature came creeping through the opening. Her mind shook her awake, yelling at her to wake Pery; that he would know what to do. No matter how much she wanted to, her muscles refused to release and she was frozen in place, forced to watch the thing creep closer in a stealthy silence a predator might use on his prey. It came within a foot of the two, towering over them, testing them and waiting. Aurora closed her eyes and forced herself to take shallow breaths, waiting for the pouncing blow. It poked her.

Aurora's heart skipped a beat as her mind was pelted with shock. She waited again. Gently the creature shook her. Chillingly she turned her head towards the creature, eyes wide as she took in the sight of his glaringly pointed teeth smiling down at her.

"WHAT THE-" Pery yelled frantically as he sloppily tried to retrieve his blade secured at his side. The creature scrambled away to the far corner of the hut, where it shrank into a ball bracing itself with it's long bony hands. Pery jumped up, a firm grip on his blade, when he caught sight of the thing in the moonlight that shone through the poorly patched ceiling. The thing was ugly as sin, almost as ugly as the Aslaiks, but at least it looked like it bathed. It was lanky and tall, with skin as wrinkly as a newborn and scarred terribly along almost every visible inch. Long claw-like fingers jutted from its hands and small beady eyes were pierced shut, awaiting more abuse to which it seemed accustomed to.

"-What are you?" Aurora asked puzzled, clamming her lips shut for such rudeness on her part. She couldn't help it, curiosity often got the better of her. Pery stopped his advance and looked at his companion. For a long stretched out silence, all that could be heard was the cowardly whimpering of the strange creature. Aurora held Pery's gaze and shook her head minutely. If the thing tried to wake her instead of instantly go for a kill, then maybe it wasn't as bad as appearances demanded. She moved to approach the creature and shrunk back as it exhumed a loud hiss as it bared it's deceivingly pointed teeth. Instantly the creature recoiled in shame and mumbled a slight 'sorry' behind tight lips.

'It can speak.' Is all that formed in her head as she thought of a better way to diffuse the situation. "What's your name?"

The creature sneezed and groaned as it curled up even tighter than before, dragging its malnourished form tighter into the corner.

"… Usellia was my name, back when I had a name." It whispered solemnly, the two barely able to distinguish one rushed word from the next. "… Before the blood wars…"

Pery remained silently skeptical, observing the creature for any giveaway of lies. He had heard that name decades previous during the climax of the Great War. Isietha had a spy by that name that sold out the Queen's pregnant daughter; Aurora's mother. The rambling confusion and gossip was so torn from the truth, that Isietha disregarded the mole's word and attempted to take the other daughter in her place. Once the truth was unveiled, Isietha became so enraged that the full force of her anger boiled over the castle and took many lives by the poison that was her hatred. Word was that the mole had escaped with his life, but became horribly disfigured from his betrayal. The mole who became a mole… how felicitous.

After a handful of minutes passed without further explanation on either end, Pery backed down and feigned a much more at-ease stance, nodding to Aurora to do the same. The tension all but vanished as the two settled back down where they were laying not but three minutes previously.

"-So what brings you to my humble abode…" The creature muttered nonchalantly with a slight quiver in his tone.

Pery hesitated for a minute as he studied this odd creature that sat huddled in front of them. Maybe he wouldn't have to tell it everything, but it wouldn't hurt to tell it what they were up to.

"We be journeying across the world to bring the darkness Isietha forged to an end." He stated calmly, as though people attempted to do such a thing weekly.

The creature's eyes lit up instantly with excitement, sparkling with blissful intent. Springing erect and still clutching it's legs to it's bone chest, it nearly fell over his own words as they escaped his too thin lips.

"I shall come too!" It exclaimed heartily as a dastardly smile crossed his face, making Aurora cringe back a bit. "-can't wait to give that demon what fer."

The two looked at one another indecisively, Aurora shrugging tired shoulders and Pery releasing a mildly defeated sigh. "-Know where to get supplies, I do. Shall be back before the dawn – Wait!" It said excitedly as it disappeared as fast as it arrived. Aurora muttered how odd the night has been and curled up by the pit, yawning as she went.

"I don't know if we can trust that thing." Pery mumbled broodingly, curling up beside Aurora whom was already half asleep.

"... I'm thinking the thing won't hurt us though. It had ample time to do so when we were sleeping. Even now instead of fighting us, it's getting ready to depart with us in the morning." She stated assuredly, "... I think that he will play a big part in this little adventure of ours... I can feel it."

Pery smirked at his partner's surprising wisdom, shutting his eyes for hopefully the last time that evening.

Chapter
Twelve

The sun rose over the horizon, peaking gently into the rundown cottage. Pery and Aurora got up without a word, moaning and groaning at rickety bones and muscles from the chilly morning frost. They banked the coals to get breakfast going, a sturdy supply of greens, leaves and more greens.

"-Heiress, mind the fire while I hunt down some real food?" He asked politely, looking at his share of soggy cooked greens and leaves, "I'd rather eat a rabbit than partake of its food…"

Aurora hid a smirk as she piled another small log onto hungry flames. An addicting melody fell from her lips into the stillness of the cottage, bringing back memories of days long passed of her friends and mother; the parties and laughs shared the familiar sights and sounds and smells of home, now just a fast fading memory.

"-What I wouldn't give to be home right now…" She whispered longingly to herself, words bouncing solidly off the walls, making it seem even more hollow and lonely. "… Have a nice hot bath, with bubbles and candles… and twilight." Talking to herself seemed foolish, but made her sanity more graspable. She missed grilled cheese sandwiches and canned mushroom soup, she missed her stuffed rabbit that no one but her mother knew she still slept with to stave off the nightmares… and her Ma, she missed her Ma most of all.

"Morrow, Puella!" Cried an overly enthusiastic, rough voice from the doorway. Aurora rushed to wipe away the tears that betrayingly had escaped her prior notice. The creature Usellia stood there, almost vibrating with excitement with arms brimming with a random assortment of things. Clumsily, it spilled the lot into a large pile on the floor in front of the now sputtering open flames.

"So, Puella, so? Where is the Putus?" It asked, becoming more fidgety and cautious by each syllable.

"Pery..." She stated the name sternly, almost positive that he was calling names, "Has gone hunting."

"Pery... as in Peregrith?" He spoke slowly, as if recalling an old past life. "I've heard that name before..." Aurora stoked the fire with a thick long stick by the wall, leaving Usellia think quietly to himself, head out in the vast yonder. She glanced over to the pile of goodies their new companion had fetched. Evidently it was still planning to go too.

Aurora was surprised to see the vast thoughtfulness put into his selections. Everything from thick woollen coats and boots to jewel laden goblets that would fetch a warlord's ransom. She recognized the carvings etched into the goblet and realized that this creature braved the City of Death for these goods. She would definitely be thinking twice on how harmless he could be.

"-To be traded for goods." He stated with a smirk, as if recalling some inside joke. A bath! Aurora thought with all her might. A bath would definitely be nice!

"Aury, you wouldn't believe what I snar-" Pery stopped dead at the sight of Usellia, leaving a beat of uneasy silence in the damp room. "-I, uh, ok... Rabbit... I culled a rabbit!" He said at last with a triumphant grin, holding up the dead creature by the ears. The damn thing was almost as big as he was! Usellia stared at the carcass then at the boy, a mildly impressed expression crossing the creature's face.

They were on the road by noon, properly clothed and amiably

stocked for the wild terrain ahead. Pery stuck to Aurora's side like glue, giving their new travelling companion cautious glances every five steps or so. The creature Usellia swathed himself in what looked to be some sort of priestly garb, covering most of his being in the thickly woven fabric apart from his obviously inhuman face. Aurora received a voluptuous overcoat lined with fur the likes of which she had never seen before, while Pery was given a similar gift of a deep grey ionar lined of the same beast. Though the creature had bore them gifts for the journey, an uneasy feeling still clung to the back of their throats; a panicky flutter of nerves that seemed to increase the further they strode down the trail.

Large outcroppings of trees overtook the vast expanse of brush and rock. An unnerving stillness clutched the heart of the woods, no animals stirred and sang their daily chatter, no breeze sifted through the branches, no outward sound called forth the knowledge of a forest except the crunching of the dried leaves echoing below their feet. A sense of cold dread clung to Aurora's chest as a musty earthy smell wafted by, making her jerk instinctively back and halt her strides. She recognized the scent and it brought a cold sweat to her brow.

It was the same scent as in the cave.

...bàs dlúthaich...

The ancient tongue whispered through her mind as Aurora frantically looked around her. Pery unsheathed his blade and followed her lead, staring at the darkness that was beginning to envelope around them, suffocating them with their own fear. Eyes began to glow within the cloak of darkness.

...bàs dlúthaich...death approaches...

Aurora's heart skipped a beat as her shaking hand found her hidden blade. Darkness and its minions crept ever so slowly towards them, smiling their shadowed fangs and snapping their razor sharp teeth as they circled their prey. Death was indeed right before them.

...bris fosgail a'balla è máji...break open the shield...

A faint feeling of déjà vu clung to her quivering thoughts as she spoke the ancient words aloud.

Wrong... It felt all too wrong.

As soon as the last syllable was uttered, everything fell away. The sheer increase in noise and light took all three aback as the deadly eyes that had circled them earlier gave form to the monsters that now encased them as their prey. Giant wolves now circled the dazed travellers as they glared into the frightened eyes of their entrapped prey. Muscles rippled along their bones as they skulked from side to side, baring brutally sharp teeth and vocalizing their excitement in the form of deep vibrating snarls. All seven of these beasts bore the camouflage of the forest with the size and no doubt strength of a small bear. An intelligent twinkle shone in the eye of the largest as it looked to the attentions of the others. These were no mere beast... these were hunters.

The first pounced at Pery, darting and dodging around his blade as it taunted him and swerved just out of range. Another snapped its massive jaw at Usellias arm, grazing the forearm with its pointed eyetooth, creating a gauntlet of blood that began to pool into his palm. Aurora's heart fell to her feet when she noticed one slowly making its way towards her, savouring the fear that it had obviously brought out full tilt in the girl. Its great paws slapped the bared earth beneath it as it grinned in mock victory. Aurora coward; she could do little else in the face of this giant predator that was soon towering a mere foot away. Its breath wreaked of blood and decayed flesh as it travelled lovingly down Aurora's neck. The hilt of her hidden blade warmed her palm as she waited for the killing blow. Within her grasp the blade grew hot and without a seconds hesitation she released the hungry blade to feed upon the hunter's mighty flesh, carving a wide gash along the jugular of the massive beast. Aurora was caught in the force of the blow and dragged down with the wolf as its spastic limbs sought to run from the danger. Blood sprayed the ground and the girl that lay amidst it, coating them in a grisly scene of death and anger.

A roar echoed through the trees that would echo a lion's murderous cry. With another breath, Aurora lept from the ground to attack the beast to her right, taking it firmly by the scruff of its gigantic neck and shoving her dagger as deep into the beasts back as she could. The wolf bucked and tumbled to the ground, pinning Aurora beneath it as the last vestiges of its breath left its body.

Aurora looked up from the shelter of the fallen beast and into the knowing gaze of the last wolf standing amidst the gore that was his pack. Panic flooded Aurora as she followed the beasts gaze to the backs of her comrades. To her utter astonishment, instead of attacking, the creature faded into the protection of the woods and vanished out of sight.

The hidden dagger fell from Auroras fingertips as the last of her adrenaline waned. Her name rang in her ears as Pery's voice began to fade from thought; from consciousness and reality.

◆——————————————◆

The world refocused into view as Aurora spastically bolted upright from her perch. Someone had dragged her to the shelter of a giant oak, protecting her if there was another deadly ambush. She watched in silence as her comrades made certain all the beasts were indeed dead. It sunk in slowly that she had killed at least one of them, and that the most powerful of the pack had walked away unscathed.

She had killed one.

Taken its life with the flick of her hand.

Blood marred her veil of innocence as it clung to her quivering flesh. The ease to which she took a life, even though it was a situation of kill or be killed, still left her feeling unclean and deadly. She had done it without thought; a reflections of memories long forgotten. What was it about that blade that she kept hidden from the world? What was her mind not telling her?

"Think we ought to save the meat?" Pery said quietly as he began skinning one of the wolves.

"Putus, there's no time-sun is going to set soon and we need to cross that river before nightfall." Usellia muttered back as he limped over to the cloak that had been torn from him during battle.

"… Surely there's enough-"

"This forest comes alive with a lot more than those little fur-balls when the sun sets." Usellia exclaimed between clenched teeth, "We need to be across the waters before that happens…" Pery glanced at the stern disfigured face as he sought for any telling of a betrayal; a bead of sweat rolled down the creatures face as the fear began to sink in. The boy nodded minutely and turned to gather their equipment, nearly mowing over Aurora in his rush.

"- Good Goddess, you're alright!" Pery nearly roared at her as he latched onto both her arms, more to steady himself than her. Staring at a silent princess, neither men spoke a word for fear it would bring on hysterics. An empty silence ensued as each looked at the other, expecting something that wasn't quite there yet. Confusion set in and Aurora was left glancing sidelong at Pery who in turn motioned to Usellia, whom wasn't paying the least bit of attention to either of them as he picked at his ghoulish nails with a small stick.

"… I'm alright…" Aurora muttered slowly, as though they were working out one of the big world mysteries.

"… Oh good, myself as well…" Pery muttered back, just as slowly. Usellia sighed deeply and mumbled a nearly indecipherable 'And you both are killing me' as he handed Aurora her pack.

"River?… Crossing?… Vastly important to your health and most likely survival?!" He exclaimed sarcastically as he began clearing some grown in shrubbery off the beaten trail, motioning for them to follow.

"-Are you sure you're ok?" Pery muttered warily as he lessened his grasp from Aurora's arms. Aurora nodded and moved to follow the path their guide had been so thoughtful as to create. Pery swallowed hard and tried to take a couple deep breaths. He knew what that woman was capable of, knew what lurked in the depths of her subconscious and her blood. He had seen her face when that monster fell beneath her feet, and prayed to the Goddess that she would be able to control the cold rage lurking beneath the surface before it grew to consume them all.

The forest closed in around them as they tried to navigate through the tangle of roots and vines that snaked in and around their ingrown path. Every step they took brought them further into a mass of dark, humid, suffocating air that could make a saint freak out. Aurora was just about to give her big comparative spiel about Tolkien's Mirkwood Forest, when the distant tell tale sounds of rushing water made its way to their ears.

Usellia grunted with satisfaction as what Aurora and Pery thought might be a bubbling brook, fell into view as an expansive, deep rush of terror. Aurora gave an internal sigh that could knock down a tower, while Pery gave a verbal equivalent to what each one was now feeling. No way on God's green earth were they going to cross that thing alive!

Dirt and sweat clung to each of them like a second skin as they pushed on down the banks of the pounding river. Exhaustion seemed to be at the forefront of everyone's mind as their feet began to drag in the fine-powdery sand. Aurora scanned over their latest obstacle, wishing desperately that difficult quests didn't involve such tiresomely difficult tasks. The sun gleamed into the grooved crevice that ran along the rivers edges, leaving the dark shadows dance amidst the white froth of the rapids. Sweet smelling ruby-red blossoms the size of her thumb layered the trees on both sides, giving blissful life to the scent that rode the warm breeze. It gave her strength; energy to push forward at a breakneck pace, passed the sluggish companions that were holding her back.

Pery watched Aurora lope past him, sighing like a little girl over a new found kitten. "What are you doing?" He muttered with brows knit tightly together, watching as she began skipping far ahead of them, giggling childlike at nothing in particular. The girl looked as high as a kite!

"Hah, look at her! She's vibrating!" Usellia exclaimed gleefully, frowning over at Pery whom looked gloomier than ever.

"Let's race, Pery!" Aurora exclaimed from up ahead, a huge grin lining her blissful face. Before he could even reply to the ridiculous comment, she tore off; bolting down the sand bars and kicking up a cloud of fine sand as she went. Pery muttered an expletive as they went chasing after the crazy drugged up princess, giggles of glee drifting back to them as the girl bound on. Calling after her and trying to keep up, the three finally managed to catch their breath as they almost ran into Aurora standing on the left bank where the river immediately forked in two.

"… I… Think… I… Won!" Aurora exclaimed between breaths, clutching the stitch in her side as her heart beat wildly against her heaving chest.

After their ears adjusted to the silence of the area, their gazes finally took in what their overworked minds refused to process. The river, which only moments ago was rushing aggressively passed them began to slow to a crawl in front of their very eyes. The left leg grew shallow and quiet where logically it should have flowed faster because of the steep decline a couple hundred meters up. If it weren't for the fact that the sun had already set upon the tree line, Usellia would have insisted on finding a better crossing further up.

The sun became a great orange disc on the barred horizon as Pery indecisively tried to reason out what was happening in front of his eyes. "-What happens when night falls here?"

The creature looked at him blankly, glancing cautiously

towards the trees, trying to hide a face of fear. "… The Ghosts come out."

Pery scoffed at the creatures fear, but worried at ignoring the warning in his eyes. A chill ran down Aurora's spine as the blissful feel-good emotions she was experiencing were instantly replaced with dread.

"-They're evil vindictive things that hunt in the night; shadows of times long past. You do not want to be caught in there world, trust me." Usellia muttered darkly as he slunk passed the two, patiently scanning up ahead for another way to cross. Dread hung in Aurora's guts as she realized that the place she stood seemed to be expelling the water away from her presence; that the river began to flow around her feet instead of through her stance. Pery caught the sense of shock in her face as he glanced over his shoulder to reveal his worst nightmare. A wall of water as tall as a two story building was rushing towards them at breakneck pace, threatening to swallow them whole.

'Across the river, we must get across!' Aurora bolted from the shoreline, away from the frantic flailing of Pery's protective clutches and into the centre of the Rivers mighty fist. She knew she could cross the ford in seconds, but the river was much faster. Like diving into an Olympic sized pool without knowing how to break the surface, the water hit Aurora hard, dragging and scraping her against the rocks and weathered driftwood, strangling the breath out of her as it pulled her further down. Voices swarmed her head, voices she didn't recognize and couldn't understand; they were suffocating her, blocking out all thoughts of escape. Her chest burned, but she didn't want to drown; didn't want to let go… not yet.

Time seemed to slow, she could see the last of the sun rays vanish behind the horizon. She could hear the jumble of voices in her head becoming softer, quieter. The pain in her chest became less apparent, the world drifting by as everything began to glow white. Peaceful… so peaceful and final.

"Aurora-No!" Pery yelled out, trying to grasp her before the wave released its fury. His cries were silenced as a rush of water engulfed his lungs. Tumbling only for a moment, he felt a sharp tug upon his coat as he breathlessly tried to reach his princess as she was carried down into the depths of a churning mass of rapids. Pery soon realized passed his sheer bewilderment that something was trying to drag him from the hungry waters onto what was left of the flooded banks.

"- Let me go, Usellia!" He screamed wildly, clawing madly with the swift currant.

"Be still yah slippery Putus! We will find her on foot, boy-We must!"

Pery glared at the creature as his senses slowly began to come back. Usellia quickly released his companion and took an uneasy step back at the sight of his enraged gaze. Something in the boys eyes formed a warning in Usellias eyes as carefully helped the lad to his feet. Filthy from the clay bank and soaked through, both of them wished for the comfort of a roaring fire, but dared not leave their quarry to the dangers of the night. A look of persistent agreement flowed between them as they silently raced on after their comrade, unawares of exactly what they will have to face once the last rays of sunlight leaves the stark horizon in twilight.

Chapter
Thirteen

'Aurora…. Aurora, sweety don't give up now.' Echoed a voice as clear as water. It was so familiar, yet so distantly tucked within her memories of a life long passed. 'Awe, Mom, but it's so hard- they won't pass me the ball… I hate soccer!' That was her back when she was seven, before her world got turned inside out. She recalled how lonely and angry she felt towards her classmates as they would pass the ball from one person to the next, always missing her when she was wide open. The feelings of lonely abandonment came flooding back, and consequently, what her mother had told her.

'There are people in this world that take pride in stealing happiness from others, my dear. Take what feelings you have right now and label them as being unfair. Know that you don't have to feel so helpless and alone as long as there is another that labels it as such. Fight against the unfairness and know that you can bring happiness to those that have lost hope. Just try… try and don't let go.'

Aurora burst out of the tumbling waters up into the blissful open air, just as the river currant dragged her under again. With an unexpected lurch, a plume of water jetted her roughly above the frothy waves, tossing her on to the damp banks in a puddle of sunken bramble. She coughed and sputtered weakly, her body aching in every joint and her lungs burning painfully from inhaling so much spray. Slowly she crawled out of the little pool, collapsing upon a frond of scraggly ferns. Aurora lay there amidst the shelter of the surrounding trees for some time, listening to the steady flow of the homicidal river not three feet beside her and wondering why on earth the damn river had just spat her out like a bad vegetable.

Trying to calm her rasping breath, she silenced every waking nerve to listen for any signs of impending danger. Just because the river hadn't claimed her, didn't mean that something else wouldn't. Her thoughts snapped to her friends and meddled about with the troublesome questions of whether they made it out alright. Was the river as generous with them as it was with her?

Laying on her side, looking up through the gap of the trees she saw a sky smitten with little speckles of light. There were stars, but there was no sign of the moon.

'But the moon was full just last night...' She thought bewilderingly to herself. Trying to stand with her seized muscles was nerve-wrecking when trying to be silent, but quickly fell low on her list of priorities as she caught a glimpse of a faint glow cascading through the forest towards her, followed by a handful of others. Suddenly, the lack of sound registered in her mind and Usellias warning became clearer; There were things in this forest one should avoid at all costs, and those things seemed to know she was there.

Aurora bolted like a frightened doe further into the woods, trying to follow the vague outline of an animal trail that led away from the waters edge. Bright silhouettes of people with long hollowed faces began to appear all around her, each more murkier and darker of light tan the other. They each shone darkness and cold about them, as if in the form of their own shadowed light. Luckily their ghastly appearances did not give them speed as she darted and dodged passed them all, afraid to touch any of them for fear of a soul-deep contamination.

Minutes melded into one another as she bolted blindly through the forest, praying she would find something she could hide under or climb up. Ghosts couldn't climb, could they? To Aurora's astonishment and utter disbelief, she had ran full circle to the bank of the same river she had been running from, only to find a very real bridge joining the two banks. Her head dizzy, from all the running she almost ran right through a spirit as it appeared a mere foot in front of her nose as she touched the first brick underfoot. Skidding to a stop, she gazed at the spectre as it stood before her. Clear definitive featured marred the darkened figure as a sense of hatred and sadness radiated all around it. Aurora could feel the eerie gazes of the dead fall upon her as they stopped their approaches. The spectre's features did not change, but from its lips she could hear it cry vengeance against a long deceased foe.

It lunged for her with a long impossibly sharp blade it morphed from the surrounding darkness. Slashing wildly at her belly, all Aurora could think to do was dodge to the sides and stay out of range. The ghosts closed in if Aurora stepped too far from the arena, jostling her forward from the excitement of fresh blood. She swayed to the left away from the creatures second blow which had just grazed her dress, leaving a slice of red fabric to dance in the whirlwind of otherworldly energy. Clutching her stomach in pain, she dodged each oncoming strike, her heart pounding in her ears as the adrenaline finally began to kick in.

The sounds of unseen swords and blood curdling cries of anguish and victory erupted as the fight marched on and Aurora's strength began to wane. Ducking around another heavy blow, she could feel herself becoming weaker from the loss of blood the opposition managed to claim from her. Her attention wavered as the brilliance of another ghost caught her eyes. One second is all the spectre needed to thrust its dark blade through the right of Auroras stomach. A yell of satisfaction erupted from the creature of its hard earned victory, before a vast column of light erupted mercilessly from its skull.

The bright apparition carelessly flung the fading ghost aside and caught Aurora as she fell to her knees. Weightlessly cradling her like a child, the ethereal being seemed to float across the rest of the bridge onto the other side and, despite the fact of an otherworldly battle waging all around them, placed her upon a massive smooth rock covered in delicate moss. Rushing to remove the patch of garment that hid the wound that burned so sharply, the apparition began whispering words of confusion and panic. Aurora winced at the pressure the warrior applied to her, as its hands sank into her skin and began to glow a soft green with magic.

"We are not of the same world Heiress, but I know who you are, and what you mean to yours. By healing your soul you can one day free mine." Aurora closed her eyes and tensed up as she could feel the last of her spirit heal. She could vaguely hear the rustling of leaves overhead and the morning larks calls to portent the suns rising.

Aurora felt a set of warm hands cup her clammy cheeks. As she opened her eyes she looked into the face of her doppelganger; The warrior was a mirrored image, with the same chocolate brown eyes and crooked smile. It was uncanny, even disturbing, yet somehow Aurora felt that she knew this spirit, this great warrior that will be locked in battle for all eternity.

"I'm glad I have known you, Aurora." She stated finally with a smile on her beautiful face. A ray of sunlight crossed the horizon and reached out to caress the warrior. The echoes of battle slowly subsided, fading into what remained of the night. The opaqueness of the warrior began to turn transparent as the suns rays clawed at her essence.

"Travel south to the old mill. Your companions have sought for you this passed fortnight and will be lodged there still..."

"-Please don't leave me!" Aurora whispered hurriedly. Doubts began to wash over her at the thought of being alone. The woman simply smiled and took Auroras quivering hands. The iridescent figure before her condensed into a fog of glistening light and faded into the morning sun.

Aurora lay still against the trunk of a huge leech tree, shaken and exhausted beyond reason. What kind of magic takes her through time and space? If that spirit really was who she thought it was, then why on earth was she there now instead of fading into the light like a bad cliche? Had she really been gone for such a long time, swept up in the bizarre magics of this world? The thundering sounds of battle had all but disappeared, leaving a lulling melody of what nature offered. Auroras fingers ran along the sheath that housed her precious dagger. She had been afraid to wield the thing before, knowing that she wasn't skilled enough to use it properly. Gently she pulled it from the scabbard and examined it with new eyes. The little blade glistened happily in the morning light, beads of blue metal twinkling like millions of little stars, whispering occult words into her thoughts. She had no excuses left, promising herself to apprehend the skills necessary for survival. It seemed that no matter where she turned, the magic of this world was staring her blazedly in the face, startling her to no end.

Wearily she stood, knees threatening to give way at any second, and tried to get her bearings. She heard the distant rushing of the same river that tried to drown her what seemed like only an hour ago. Dragging herself to the rive bank, Aurora peered out through the edge of the treeline, half expecting the wall of water to appear threateningly before her once more. It was no longer a rush of foaming typhoons that threatened to engulf any creature attempting to disturb its waters. Aurora shook her head in bewilderment at a family of small deer drinking at the shore not ten feet in front of her. Two of the young ones danced and frolicked about the others playfully, disturbing a shining speck from the shoreline with their tiny hooves.

Curiosity rushed through her as she crept closer to investigate. The animals scurried back into the cover of the forest as Aurora approached the spot she had seen the glimmer of shining metal. Kneeling down and picking up the piece of metal, Aurora soon recognized the hinged oval shape of an old locket, heavily worn from years of wear and fondling. She turned it over in her palm, feeling every smooth cold corner it possessed, unable to sift out any outward inscription or flourishing design. It held a plain simple beauty that reminded Aurora of home. Fumbling it into a pocket as she stood, Aurora couldn't put it off any longer. She had to find that mill.

Removing her shoes, she dug her sore feet into the finely eroded sand as she walked along the bank. The sun beat upon the sand grains below as the tree blossoms fell into luscious bloom. There wasn't a single breeze to ward the days heat from her sweating skin and the river beside her didn't move any faster than her steady forward gate. Despite the hunger and weariness she felt, Aurora actually began to feel almost content. Even without the lack of sure-fire protection and the company of two vastly different souls to kill the time, the fact that nothing was chasing her, trying to maim her, or kill her made her more relaxed than she had been the last month.

She stayed on the west side of the river, winding in and around the forest. It wasn't until well into the afternoon that Aurora caught sight of the mill, tucked within an outcropping of trees and boulders of blue stone that lined the now narrow river. Climbing over smooth slimy rocks to reach a trail running a couple yards parallel the river, she dragged her wearily exhausted body the last half a mile to the building in the distance.

'Will there be people there?' She began to wonder as each step slowed ever so slightly. What if people knew she wasn't from around there, and if they did, would they even care?

Shaking off her insecurities she quietly crept the last couple yards to the small building, listening for any sounds of danger as she slowly cracked open the door. To her utter relief and dismay, it was deserted. The door creaked open as she crept her way inside, examining the fine film of dust layering everything. It was one big room with the wheel attached to the northern-most wall, with various old and discarded furniture littering the floor. There was a cooking pit in the centre of the room with an old aged bed, still sturdy enough for the odd weary traveller, to her immediate left. In the corner, wedged between the bed and a flimsy table was a satchel she recognized all too well as she rushed over to dig into Pery's pack to extract as much food as she could stuff into her face without throwing up. Her insides twisted with pain at being introduced with solid food once again as she clutched her stomach with a low moan.

Aurora sat there in the corner, on top of the old lumpy bed, her chin resting on her knees, as she patiently waited for the exact second that her friends would walk through that door. Each moment turned into ten, then a hand full more and still there was no sign of her companions. As the minutes ticked by with no more than the sound of the wind whistling through the drafty corners of the mill and the random chirping and singing of little animals just outside the thin walls, Aurora's eye lids closed and fell into a deep slumber that the end of the world would not succeed to wake her from, with only one thought left on her mind... *What happened to her Peregrith?*

⊷Peregrith⊷

He saw her being pulled under the raging waters, yet couldn't do anything to stop it. Usellia held him back from the riptides of the angry river, long bony hands entwined in Pery's soaked shirt.

"Let me go!"

Usellia shook his head at his friend and held firm as he lost sight of Aurora. He knew that it was a trap; knew that something was amiss when the river had slowed it's brisk pace at the mere disturbance of its shore. It settled upon his gut like sharp stones that he had failed to protect her yet again and couldn't help but imagine her chilling image drowned and floating along the bottom of the rapids, or being smashed to pieces against the jagged rocks he had just escaped from himself. The haunting images stirred emotions in him he hadn't felt in eons and immediately suppressed them so as not to fall victim to his own inner demons.

"Come Boy, we will find her down river." Usellia spoke solemnly into the densely devastated air.

They went for hours along the weathered river banks looking for their princess. Pery was scared senseless to find her lying lifeless against the banks, or worse yet, not at all. Travelling as far as an abandoned mill, they set up camp. Hunting and patrolling along the banks for any sign of her during the day, and barring themselves inside the shack at night. The sounds of a ferocious battle echoed through the thick forest when twilight broke, leaving the two to sit there most of the night and wait for the sun to rise once more.

"Do you think she's dead?" Usellia asked softly, staring out across the river at the family of deer stopping to drink. Pery glanced briefly at his unseemly companion, not really seeing the creature in front of him. He had asked that same question at least a hundred times throughout those excruciating weeks. Fifteen days and nights had drifted by with no sign of their quarry. Game was becoming scarce and very soon, they would have to unwillingly move on down the river.

"… We will find her." Pery whispered more to himself than Usellia. The creature sighed lightly and rose from his perch, ready to scour the riverbanks for clues for the umpteenth time that week. With a heavy heart, Pery followed. Every day at noon they would reach an old weathered bridge, half crumbled into the rushing waters and that's where they would part ways, one to hunt supper, and the other to continue scouring the banks for the body of a princess.

Pery was blindly gazing across the waters into the parallel tree-line when something shifted and caught his eye. Fading into the stillness of the trees, a figure stood within shadows, ghostly in appearance; iridescent and unmoving like only the dead can put across to the living, but lacking the hollowness that a ghost would exhibit within their eyes. Pery immediately thought the worst as the figure became more distinctive and solid, though something about this ghost threw him off-kilter, as though he were looking at the future version of his beloved heiress. Pery glanced over to an oblivious Usellia whom was exploring the nearby grumble-berry bush and came to wonder why he was the only one to sense the spectres presence.

A heavy warmth filled the air as Pery realized he was staring into an empty void of space and time. Then he felt her. Wrapped loving and protective hands around him, whispering memories of what never passed into his strained ears. Pery couldn't breathe for fear of chasing her away, this spectre that looked so much like his princess. The sweet scent of geranium wrapped around his senses and he could almost see her smile at him through the veil of time. That's what she was… Aurora's future self. A great warrior in every right and still as gentle and beautiful as the first day he laid eyes on her. As real as this memory felt to him, he knew that she was not real to this world, not yet; just a faint impression within the veil of time. She wasn't real, but her wordless message was.

'I found her, my Peregrith-I found her after all this time... I... finally...'

The river's mist swallowed up his precious princess, leaving him with a hollow feeling of being robbed of all senses. Coming back to reality he realized what the spectre had told him. Hope began to fill his soul once more.

⤛Usellia⤜

Usellia had no idea what was going through his comrade's head as the boy stood out in the open, staring at the space to the creatures right. He reminded Usellia of the one time he came across a wondrous ring of luscious mushrooms that he simply couldn't abandon. The resulting hallucinations and tasting of colours left Usellia to believe they were the stepping stones to the world of the Fey, which seemed to be the case for his dear friend, Pery, whom had found himself right in the middle of such a fairy ring. Laughable to say the least to the boys comrade, but not all that harmful.

It was when Pery began making his way back to the mill that Usellia thought the better of it. Having little choice but to follow the staggering boy, so drunk with the tingling Fey magic he could almost taste it in the air, they stumbled back the way they had come.

He could feel it, the dragging sensation that his gut made when he himself had no clue what was happening. He could hear Usellia trailing close behind, muttering odd remarks about drugs and firing cannons while inebriated.

'She's alive... she's alive and will be there.' He thought to himself severely, practically running back towards the mill.

Bursting through the door, he scanned the dust laden shell of a cottage but found not a living soul within its confines. His heart sank to his knees as the adrenaline seeped out of his body, leaving him feel heavy and weak upon his feet. Maybe his mind was finally leaving him, just maybe-

"Peregrith…" Muttered a breathy voice directly behind them. Pery and Usellia turned in unison and feasted their gazes upon an oily and dirt laden woman with arms full of fire wood. She was all but a dishevelled mess, with patches of dried blood here and there and dirt marring her fine features. With a low whimper of disbelief, the small twigs fell to the ground and Aurora embraced her dearest friends, tears rushing down her dirt ridden cheeks. A rush of relief like anything he had ever felt rushed through Pery as he clutched her firmly, not caring that she was drenching his cloak in silent tears.

"-Okay friends!" Usellia squeaked breathlessly, trying to squirm out of Aurora's painful embrace. "The berries…" Aurora immediately let go, now smelling the clump of berries that were staining the creatures cloths. Pery gathered the forgotten pile of firewood that lay at their feet as Aurora quickly prepared a feast fit for a king as her unruly belly echoed through the mill. Soon they were stuffing their faces, sitting contently by the roaring pit, warmth encircling them all for the first time in what seemed like eons. After chatting their way long into the night, they all began to drift into dreams of ice cream and rose petals, and in Usellias case, a bracket full of deliciously plump and yummy bugs ripe for the eating. Pery couldn't decipher the paradox of emotions that ran through his weary body as he nodded off to sleep. Watching the soft flames before them licking the air above it, tasting it's rich coolness upon it's searing tongues. Whatever these odd feelings were, where so ever they might eventually lead, he was eternally happy to just have his friend back in one piece

.

◄◄Usellia►►

Usellia woke with a start, eyes snapping wide open at a sound outside the door. The predawn light peaked over the horizon, resting upon the sill that faced the river. He sat still as the growl of a hungry mountain lion patiently purred directly on the other side of the door. Pery and Aurora lay peacefully beside him, still safe and sound in their dreams. Silently he thanked the goddess that the door was as strong as it was, but knew he still needed to get rid of the beast before his companions stirred it into a frenzy. Without hesitation, Usellia grabbed on of the daggers he had found for them and crept out of the opposite window. The morning air was brisk and the dew clung to his feet purposely, stealing the last bits of heat the warm fire had gifted him with. The birds had just started to stir and sing their morning cheer. Within all the commotion of the waking world, Usellia crept silently around the building.

In the shadows before the door, sitting amidst the dry bristle that had been piled inside the mill, perched a feline nearly thrice the size of himself. It's golden coat glistened in the light of the rising sun, tail twitching to and fro with anticipation for its prey. Usellia had only one shot to take the beast down and by the looks of it's scarred flesh scattered all over its body, many have tried and failed. Centring himself with a silent deep breath, Usellia lept for the kill, feeling every fleeting moment slowly creep by. With one hand he held fast to the scruff of fur at the back of it's neck while simultaneously plunging the blade up to the bejewelled hilt into it's jugular. It stumbled upon it's own tracks and soon lay twitching upon the dust strewn earth, blood gurgling around its cries of muted anger. Not but a minute later, the grisly sound of the blade sliding from the flesh of a fresh kill made his stomach churn deep within his guts. No matter how many times he had killed or will ever kill for survival or sustenance, he would never get used to that gut wrenching sound. That aside, he took a quick step back to analyze his kill.

The creature, still flinching from such an instantaneous death, lay before Usellia. Being twice as long and thrice as muscular, he was beginning to wonder on the ease of such a kill. The scars to which seemed irrelevant before now seemed to glow with importance, revealing something hidden deep within his vast memories; creatures that one should not attempt to claim in death. A cold rippling sweat perspired upon Usellia as the recollection settled itself upon his brow.

Forest guardians were forbidden to be taken.

A crackling of dried leaves echoed through the now painfully quiet forest, creating a gut wrenching feeling in the pit of his very soul. The birds that had begun to wake fell silent upon the forest spirits presence. Usellia refused to look upon its wonder, feeling the ghosts presence a mere three feet ahead of him. Eyeing the beast he had just slew so carelessly he swore to himself over and over for his stupidity.

"Why have you slain my guardian, Protector?" The ghost whispered in a quiet trance-like cadence. "My home is now without a warrior and I seek recovenance for this sin."

Usellias throat grew dry and rough, leaving his voice to quiver a harshly rough reply, "... It was to protect my friends." Gazing upon the ashen face of the beast, all he wanted at that moment was to turn back time and not have woken that morning. "-What can I do...?"

Silent as a shadow, the spirit wisped to kneel before the beast, shocking Usellias senses as he unwillingly laid eyes upon the magic of the forest. The spirit was clad in trees and leaves, or was one with them Usellia was not sure. Its eyes were that of flowers and the peak of light from the confines of rain-clouds. Shifting from one form to another, the spirit held fast to it's personification of Mother Natures living children. It held no gender and possessed a voice of bluebells blowing in a morning breeze. Suddenly, Usellia would have done anything to appease this spirit whom dared show itself in a way few others ever have in this age. Usellia was both relieved of it's boldness and unsure of whether it meant harm to them all. Thinking over to where his friends still lie asleep and innocuous of his sin, he could only pray that this spirit was truly benevolent.

"From the ashes of my guardian and the blood of the slayer, might I have his soul back within my power." Usellia flinched at the mention of blood, particularly with the departure of his blood. "- But i have no power over mortal beings..."

Usellias heart skipped a beat. He wasn't going to be forced

into anything, but watching the spirit coo the dead beast in an anguished tone, he knew that it needed to be done.

As quickly as he could, Usellia built a small fire beside the creature and dragged its massive body to the centre, careful not to smother the hungry flames. He watched as the spirit swayed this way and that like the limbs of a tree in the wind. Taking the dagger he had used on the beast, he slowly ran the sharp blade across the flesh of his palm. A pool of fresh blood welled up in his hand as he held it cupped over the flames. The spirit spoke words of an old tongue, long forgotten by mortal minds. His blood began pulsing and glowing an iridescent bright red, becoming filled with a humming vibration of magic that vanished as suddenly as it had begun.

Within a heartbeat the fire consumed beast and that of its master had vanished, leaving Usellia to stand alone in the wake of the embers that remained behind. He suddenly felt exhaustively cold and lonely, wishing nothing more that he could be in that drafty mill, safely warm and sleeping.

Slowly he strolled to the river's edge and cleared his skin of all the blood, noticing a faint outline of the mark his blade had made, now completely sealed and shaded a peculiar green. Marked by old magic... how lovely.

Chapter
Fourteen

The day formed grungy around them, dark clouds threatening an already dark horizon and the smell of a cold rain hung in the air. A chill ran through Aurora as the wind tried to creep beneath the folds of her clothing. Clutching her cloak tightly around her neck, she strode stiffly behind her two companions, wishing for much better protection than a stupid dress would ever permit. Pery acting all the man, tried not to draw blood as he almost bit his tongue off from the bitter frigidness of the morning air.

The nearest settlement was due north, following the curvature of a rapturously high cliff that plummeted at a 90 degree angle some 300 feet to the river below. Rough winds and sideways rain whisked the travellers mighty close to the edge as they clung on to any rooted thing they could get their numb mitts on, which was thinning with every step they took. By night fall, the painfully thin, cracked lips of their alien friend mumbled and pointed to a sheltered crevice along the tree-line. The last rays of sunlight sunk below the horizon as the three of them carefully made their way into the man-made cavern, moving as silently as their creaking bones would allow. Pulling the same blue orb Pery had used what seemed like eons past, the walls came alive with the shimmering magics of dear old Kanna. A stabbing pain rushed through Aurora's gut at the memory of the old Hag, blind yet all seeing and all heart. Why couldn't her Grandmother have been like that...

Along the side of the wall lay a stack of dry firewood with an assortment of clay jars and stone boxes and a thick carpet of fine moss that looked more comfortable than a sleepy fat puppy.

"The main merchants that travel the highway just a couple yards up set up this place so they could have a safe place to rest." Usellia muttered as he set up an odd metal tripod over the fire and motioned to the stone boxes along the wall. " Could you bring me the pot and what not Heiress, this fire's still hungry." Aurora obliged curiously as she instantly found a small cast-iron cooking pot with wooden bowls and utensils. Handing the pot to Usellia who had it attached and waiting within minutes, Aurora continued probing the supplies that seemed so out of place to be just lying around in a hole in the ground.

"How is it that no one has taken any of this stuff?" Aurora mumbled, more to herself than either of the party.

"There's a spell on everything; It can't leave the opening of the cavern. If you press the little circle on the surface of those boxes, there should be dried goods and a white powder to chase away the shivers." Glancing over at Pery who gave a small shrug as he went back to unpacking the bedrolls, Aurora grazed her finger over the perfectly etched circle upon the top of the stone boxes and almost fell over as it popped open and folded out to be three times the size as it should have been. She thumbed through the sacks of grains and dried berries, finding the white powder Usellia was hinting towards. Each item was clearly labelled and patiently waiting to be used. Picking out five sacks of unheard of foods, she brought them over to their chef and patiently awaited more instruction. Usellia stopped prodding the fire long enough to glance at the bags, look bemusedly over to Pery and try not to laugh as he traded three of the bags for something else.

"... It wouldn't of tasted that bad..." She stated pridefully, trying desperately not to twiddle her thumbs in embarrassment.

"-Oh It would have tasted heavenly going down... but not so much coming back up for the next three days." He stated between quiet laughs. With cheeks quickly becoming scarlet, Aurora strode over to the far corner of the cavern and huddled within herself, hiding beneath her damp cloak. Pery hid his grin as he began hanging up the drenched clothing on a makeshift line by the fire.

"Lass, you don't need me to tell you how new you still are at this. Just give yourself some time, it's not like either of us expects you to learn everything overnight. So buck up, keep your mind fresh and throw me your cloths so you don't catch he shivers." Pery was right and she knew it. Heaving a big sigh of contention, she began peeling layer after layer of clothing off, handing each article off to him and finally changing into a short thick woollen tunic that barely fell past her thighs. All possible embarrassment aside, she wandered over to Usellia to blab incoherently about how and what she would cook if she were back at home. Once past the babble, he explained in length how it was done here. Sitting around the fire, talking at length about healing practices and various technologies of each worlds, Aurora came to the conclusion that at some point, religion had replaced the ideas of alchemic science; that the supplication and restriction of her worlds beliefs to one main religion had stifled their advancements, yet made them blossom in the past three centuries. Science is the supposed understanding of Earths ways, and Magic was the use of it. Somehow the knowledge of processes became more important than being able to use them.

With a full belly and their cloths now toasty warm, they stoked the fire one more time and hit the hay with a vengeance.

* * *

I stare into the face of blissful innocence and yet still know not how I will ever let her go. One single moon cycle has passed for Goddess' sake, a mere cycle... and yet something stirs when I look her way." Pery gazed at his sleeping companion, a pained countenance marring his aura. The dim light from a dying fire flickered across her face, highlighting the golden sheen of her wavy locks. Even her dirt laden face didn't hide the magnificence owed to her by her kin's blood. Ever so gently, Pery brushed aside a stray lock of hair. His hand lingering upon her cheek, wishing he could understand the feeling that knotted his guts into aggregation. What first was an unwillingness to bother with this outsider, had turned into a burning desire to protect and help her in every way possible.

Pery recoiled his hand, his own thoughts burning him. What was he thinking? Whatever his heart may say, his mind knew otherwise. *When the end comes, no one wins... not even my silly little heart.*

<hr style="width:30%;" />

The morning arose fresh and crisp on their senses. The sun shone elegantly through the caverns mouth, painting the far wall in an expanse of lush gold and orange hues that would dance with the leaves outside. Birds singing their morning tunes and the chattering of squirrels livened up the forest.

"Can we just stay here for a couple of days?" Aurora sighed happily, stretching her hands up far over her head. Usellia grunted in blissful agreement as he soaked up the sun like a plant. *It was such a good idea to come here...*

"-I'd much rather find a bath at the next settlement. They have the best bath-house on the peninsula..." Pery wistfully muttered, leaving the three of them to sigh internally at the thought of such a luxury.

At noon Usellia put out the fire and they bid a swift farewell to their little oasis amidst such a drab journey, making their way up to the road that will lead them to Alidale.

Aurora was a-jitter with excitement at the thought of a nice relaxing bath, and the chance to hopefully find somewhere to wash her garments which were probably just as dirty as she was. As she flipped thorough the prospect of cleanliness and newly laundered undergarments, she finally caught notice to the crimson stained scarf Usellia had draped about himself from head to toe. She couldn't blame him either. In a world as different as this, those that stood out were most likely to be singled out, abused, outcast or killed. Not much unlike her own world, only slightly cruder on the execution of societies disapproval.

"Is there something you require Heiress?" Usellia asked

point-blank, startling her out of her reverie. She hadn't realized she was staring.

"I like your scarf..." She blurted out without recourse, both blushing a dangerously deep red hue. He muttered a muffled 'thanks', looking anywhere but at them. "-I'm not a bad sewer y'know." She stated to herself, causing Pery's brows to rise almost past his hairline. "Maybe I can make y'all something..." She finished shyly, twiddling her thumbs nervously as her cheeks remained marred with a faint blush.

"I'd like that." Pery caught himself saying.

"As would I!" Usellia exclaimed brightly, a twinkle flashing in his eye. Never had he had a friend offer to do anything for him, let alone someone as important as the future ruler of the nation.

"... So this is the trade route you had spoken of right?" Aurora asked.

"Aye."

"- Why aren't there more people? It's been hours and we haven't met a single one."

"Patience Aury, you spoke too soon." Pery muttered cautiously as the sound of a group of people drifted to them around the bend. The trees made it hard to see what was causing the commotion, but the sounds from ahead weren't cries of joy or pleas for happiness. Pery motioned for Aurora and Usellia to take cover. Without making a sound he vanished into the forest, presumably to save the day. After a moment, Aurora followed after him, the sounds of the strangers growing louder as she approached. She could vaguely hear Usellia behind her as she peered at the small caravan not twenty feet away. It looked to be a family of merchants, all gathered in a clump in front of their largest wagon, and blocking their way was a gang of Aslaiks terrorizing their prey. Aurora caught her breath as dread snaked down her spine, Usellia remaining as silent as the dead beside her. There were eight large disfigured monsters standing before the three women whom guarded their goods. Quiet weeping could be heard from within the canvassed wagon two wagons back, no doubt terrified of what would be to come. No men stood with their kin to guard the caravan, making Aurora second guess where they might be. Even she knew that a travelling group wouldn't go about the countryside without protection.

"-Hey Daague, cud'n I jus peck off the youn un, ay?" The smaller of the creatures lisped with a nasty sneer on its malformed lumpy face.

"Hold," The middle one said menacingly, grinning broadly at the youngest girls blanch to his uncharacteristic softness. "I got me a different plan for herrr..." The girl's eyes widened as blood drained from her face. The other creatures laughed and jeered the threat of blood and rape in their prey's faces. They loved it when their prey's blood ran a frenzied before they spilled it upon themselves, and unfortunately for them, the younger the better. The two watched in paralyzed silence as the gang loomed closer with their makeshift weapons cutting the air lazily in front of them, making the three women back up in fear. The leader prodded the girl with the hilt of his sword, taunting her into a terror that Aurora was all but feeling herself. She couldn't watch this happen; she had to do something. The buzzing in her ears readied her for the jump to redemption. God she was such a little coward. Who cares if she didn't know how to fight, she couldn't stand by while watching another innocent get killed or worse... god there was worse... all she would have to do was be quick.

Before she could bolt from her cover a flash seeped out to confront the monsters and she wouldn't have seen it if she weren't so focused on the scene in front of her. Cries of pain rang up from the two that spoke, their jugulars slashed and oozing the life blood that they so coveted. The beasts crumpled to the ground as the other creatures skittered around, trying to remain in control. Whistles rang through the air as three more dropped like a sack of potatoes, an arrow protruding from their foreheads dead centre. The remaining turned tail and bolted down the path Aurora, Pery and Usellia had just come, shoving and arguing over whom goes first.

Three burly men emerged from the cover of trees, merging with the women whom stood so bravely amidst almost assured destruction. They began talking amidst themselves as the children and a couple of older folk emerged from the protection of the wagons, the oldest of the lot motioning for Pery to come forward. Aurora hesitated within the line of trees, her legs now jelly-like from the adrenaline rush, barely able to hold herself up as Pery came casually prancing over to her, the women looking on in curiosity.

"The b'ys and me are goin' hunting. Keep with the caravan and I'll meet up with you at their home-"

"Seriously... You're just gonna dump me with a bunch of strangers?" Aurora whispered furiously.

"-I know them Aury, have known them for years as they've dealt with Kanna for generations." A faint blush crept over her cheeks at the thought of him so easily abandoning her, not after everything they've been through.

"... We must catch up to the creatures before they can gather another raiding party and hunt us down. There's no element of surprise on our side if they come back." Pery gently cupped her pale cheek, inwardly wincing at having to leave her in the hands of someone else. Usellia served as a protection, but knowing him, that protection would be in the shadows and nothing more. It was a chance for her to become a part of this world through partaking of its people. How he wished he could shield her from it forever...

Aurora soaked in the strength Pery possessed and gave a shaky, yet determined nod. Hoping to convey the bravery she so desperately wished she felt. Pery gave a faint smile before he left off from her hiding place and quickly lept to the group that had already began their hunt. Groaning inwardly she glanced around for the now missing Usellia and emerged from the bushes, hoping without hope that he would at least be around just in case. When thinking back upon Mr. Panther and that blasted map he tried to get her to memorize, she felt overwhelming panic at the thought that she didn't recall a single geographical shape from the thing. She cleared her throat as she slowly approached her new travelling companions, all of which were dressed in the same 3 shades of chocolatey brown. Their chestnut coloured hair coiled around their heads in a lovely braided crown, each one laced with varying degrees of grey depending upon their age, and to Aurora's relief, all nine of them were smiling knowingly at her.

"-Ye are welcome wit us lass, " The oldest spoke gently, a grandmotherly smile covering her face. "Though we mus leave off this momen', fer night approaches us fast in dese here parts." No sooner than the lady spoke the words the wagons began moving again, the oxen grunting with the effort and Aurora silently strolling behind.

They moved fast and kept a constant pace along the winding roads through the forest. Their path was smoothed out with blue flagstones, the same blue rocks that originated from Usellia's mighty home. Sitting on the back of the last cart with the youngest girl, she casually glanced around, hoping to catch a glimpse of a trailing Usellia hidden amidst the trees. After nearly an hour of cautious glances and non-stop babble from the optimistically enthusiastic child, Aurora answered the girl's most prominent questions about how to ride sea dragons, smiled and jumped down to walk a spurt and stretch her muscles. The road was wondrously flat and well used, being framed with a small series of fist sized smooth stones the colour of the summers sky on a cloudy day. Leaves whispered in the cool breeze, their yellow coined fingers beckoning the company through.

Most of the afternoon was filled with small chatter and the singing of local songs. Sarita, Aurora discovered was the Grandmother and leader of the merchant caravan. Together with her five children, eight grand children and her life-mate Boar, they had travelled that road for over 23 long years toting food, foreign textiles, toys and any other goods they came across along the way. It wasn't until the last hours of light that Aurora began to feel the worrisome stab of frustration at both Pery and Usellias absence.

"-Do you think they'll be alright?" Aurora asked out of the blue. Sarita's face grew kind at the young girls worry.

"Peregrith and my kin will do well in the absence of their hearts... not to mention the four of them are highly trained in the arts of the blade and arrow.

"Pery has a heart..." Aurora mumbled quietly, looking to the ground in embarrassment. She didn't have to guess what the old woman guessed. The woman softened her demeanour and gently patted Aurora's arm in care.

"-I do not mean he is cold heartless, Daughter, I mean that with the one he loves being tucked away in safety, he is free to give hunt whole mindedly." Aurora's face grew red with the woman's boldness, but didn't have the heart to argue with the kind lady.

"... And we are safe?" She asked quietly in the face of those wise eyes. A smile formed on the woman's thin mouth.

"As safe as most in a merchants caravan." The woman glanced over to Aurora's worried expression and couldn't help but pat the poor girl gently on the shoulder. "Do you know how to defend yourself, Daughter?"

Aurora shook her head. "Only a very little."

Sarita lit up with glee as she called to one of the younger women to them, a knowing smile on her face.

"Kasha, this girl doesn't know how to fight - teach her!"

The girl groaned as she looked at this hopeless lass strolling behind the last wagon. The only thing that came to Kasha's mind was 'weak' and 'tedious charity'. Her multiple braids of golden ropes of hair shifted over her face as she looked up to the sky, silently praying for deliverance from her grandmother's ongoing meddling with others' lives. Her honey brown eyes measured their temporary ward from head to toe, trying hard not to laugh aloud at the sight. This girl looked completely out of place for where they were. No muscle showed through the soft pudge that would certainly cushion her fall if nothing else, and a concerned vacant expression that had been looming over her face the entire day. This girl reminded Kasha of a half dim goat that got kicked too many times as a babe. Whoever this girl was, she needed more than a simple lesson in blades, she needed to be clued in on the ways of the world, and soon.

Aurora watched as Kasha sorted through a mess of random items hidden under a burlap sack inside one of the wagons. Rippling muscle scoured the girls arms as she pulled two long poles from the cart. Gingerly Kasha tossed one to Aurora, dismounting in one clean swoop. Aurora's throat grew dry as the girl motioned for her to follow suit. With as swift as a motion as any, Aurora slipped from the jolting cart and nearly stumbled head over heels into the fine silt.

"Don't break yourself." Kasha taunted smugly as Aurora suppressed a humiliated grunt. Kasha let the caravan go ahead while she systematically began twirling the pole amidst agile fingers. The staff became a blur as Aurora became queasy at the realization that her clumsiness is about to cause some fierce embarrassment on her part.

"Now, start slow and twirl it around your hands like this." The girl instructed, moving the pole smoothly between each finger. Aurora tried slowly and promptly hit herself in the face. Rubbing the sting away she began again, moving to catch up with the group with the girl.

As the company hid their snickers and smiles they kept on through the forest, only stopping for brief interludes of necessity when required. By the third hour, Aurora could wield the pole decently without damage to herself or those around her. A smug expression fell on Kasha at her student's progress. Neither had noticed the shadows of night creeping on them or the thinning of the trees until it appeared before them; a sprawling town of at least a miles length lay in front of their path. Nestled in the hollow of a valley sat the expanse and glory that was Tevanton. All the buildings were different than Aurora could ever imagine. The last light of the day shone down into the heart, setting it aflame with an orange fire... and it shone. Every surface that made up those buildings shimmered and glistened from the light as though the entire expanse were made of a glass or chrome. Prim gardens and controlled wildlife accented the civilized structures and sculptures that followed a circular pattern, almost like a maze, from the centre of the cluster.

It was simply breath taking.

Chapter
Fifteen

After the initial shock and awe began to subside, they began their descent down the gradual slope that led to the centre of the mass splendour. The streets were crowded with people bustling to and fro with odd decorations in their arms. As Aurora glanced around her, she came to notice various wild decorations spread across each step, doorway and window; tribal elements that didn't seem to have any place in such a prestigious community. Brightly painted stalls filled to the brim with alien objects lined the main roadway, merchants calling out the goods they presented for huge prices.

Everyone greeted the caravan as they travelled down the line, not blinking an eye to the strange girl that gawked at the wonderments around them all. Aurora clutched firmly to her pole, to which looked more like a long walking stick seeing how the townsfolk carried theirs. Everyone carried one in some form or another, either gripped tightly by gnarled and ancient fingers or hanging securely from their decorative woven cloth belts.

"Relax Shashi, you're making me nervous." Kasha mumbled , an amused look dancing in her eyes. "It's the festival tonight."

Kasha was surprised at the confusion that spread across Aurora's brow.

"-You know, the festival?... Celebration of life and death? Harvest and the lunar cycle?" Aurora's face froze into a mask of obliviousness. "Juda, what rock have you-"

"From up north... Haven't left the farm until now..."

Kasha's brows rose but she pried no further. Aurora could tell a million questions flooded the girl's mind but, for once, politeness was firmer than curiosity.

"Anyways, this festival is thrown every year after all the crops have come in." The girl gestured towards a row of tall cylos and an odd hut that had smoke coming from it's five chimneys. "It's to give thanks to the goddess for her gifts to us." The caravan halted at one of the booths and began unloading their goods onto the shelves and hammocks that hung overhead.

"Kasha, bring our guest to Anni's will you?" The mother spoke over her shoulder as she juggled a clay pot, glass bottle, and the youngest girl behind the booth. A grumbled groan escaped the girl's lips as she motioned for Aurora to follow. Grabbing her bag, Aurora hurried to keep up with the grumbling merchant girl.

Winding around the endless crowd and collection of animals, Kasha weaved her way through the busy town, not particularly caring if her charge was following or not. Aurora couldn't utter a word over all the commotion and watched as Kasha fell out of sight into a short building made of ivory brick and stone. Aurora lingered in the doorway as she scanned the room. There amidst a group of children ranging in age from 2 to adolescence, sat a plump elder lady with short, wispy white hair and skin as wrinkled as a naked mole. Her Attention drifted over to the new girl who stood nervously in her wake.

"Kasha, my child, who is this?" The old woman croaked sweetly.

"-Her name's Aury, Anni... Supposed to be related to Peregrith..." She spoke reluctantly before disappearing into the crowd of bustling family members.

The old woman's smile faltered at the mention of Pery, eyes becoming sharper as she glanced her up and down. Her mouth twitched as something in her head clicked. Aurora swallowed hard, panic flooding her mind as she tried to keep her expression plain. If old Anni had realized who she was, she didn't spit a word as she beckoned Aurora in. Kasha watching with an odd expression in the corner chair, nose firmly implanted into a thick book, grumbling as though it were a chore to have Aurora in her presence.

"So Aury... How came you to this humble town?" Anni asked, eyes sparkling mischievously. Aurora nearly choked on the finely rehearsed words she had thought of previously.

"I lived up north for most of what I remember.. It wasn't until recently that I had found out that those that raised me were not my blood kin. They told me where I was found as a child and what had become of my family. Naturally I sought it out and found my brother by sheer luck..."

Anni nodded her wise approval as her suspicions began to fade. "-And where be your heading now child?" Aurora's smile faltered, she hadn't thought that far ahead. *Such a nosy old woman.* She thought to herself. Just as Aurora was about to stumble into a tale she hoped she would be able to remember, the door swung ajar spilling more of the merchant family into the compact house. The room was booming with excitement and joy as the colourful decorations and costumes outside in the town came flooding in. All the girls beamed their child-like energy across the group, all save for Kasha, whom sat grumpily in her corner.

"Aury, are you gonna come?" One of the girls called across the room, running to her side with a half toothed grin flashing in her face. Aurora had no answer as she tried to act dignified through her unwanted refusal.

The room suddenly grew even louder as cheers of welcome rang through the building; the men had finally returned from the hunt, sacks full of treasures and giant smiles laden upon their faces. Aurora brightened as Pery stepped in behind them, all senses of worry gone from his face. The young girl that was speaking with Aurora tugged at her skirts, still awaiting her answer.

"I suppose it is up to my brother..." She finally answered. The girl broke out into an assortment of adorable giggles as she ran up to Pery. Aurora watched as the girl asked the same question to her comrade. Glancing up to Aurora, Pery raised his brows in a question. Aurora nodded slightly, trying not to break her face from smiling so much. She liked this family, feeling amazingly safe in these new surroundings. The child jeered at Pery's quick answer, tripping over herself to tell her ma and pa the exciting news.

As the sun shone it's last rays, the light from the hearth shone elegantly upon the elaborate embroidery and bead work all the women were working on. Aurora curiously watched as the elder's decrepit and arthritic hands flew around the silken cloth, leaving behind the most beautiful border along the neck-line.

"Is this your first festival, Aury?" Called a shy voice amidst the group. The question reeked of hope and as shy eyes met shy eyes, Aurora internally sighed for the deterrent of awkward silence. Aurora remembered to nod after a long minute of fluttering internal dialogue. She glanced at the girl from the corner of her eye and saw a younger version of Kasha working on a slightly different form of dress everyone else seemed to be working with.

"Tori, you know she's been living in the clouds til now, you big Shashi-"

"Kasha, what have I said about using curses, you fool of a girl!" Anni boomed from across the loose circle. Aurora inwardly laughed at the grump, happy that someone could put her in her place. "Now, Kasha, go get Aury one of the older skins to fix up." The old woman spoke gently.

"... Can't Tori go get it-"

"I asked you girl! Since you're not working on your own, may as well get our guest set up for tonight." Kasha grumbled loudly as she dragged herself to the chamber door next to her. A couple moments later, she came out with a bundle of faded but perfectly embellished cloth in her arms. The girl tossed one of them to Aurora as she plunked herself back down in her little corner. Aurora could swear there were black clouds hanging over the girls head as she settled back into her book with a grim scowl on her face.

As the women finished their additions to their skins, they passed them to the men, whom in turn, presented the women with crowns of small antlers. Everyone dawned on their skins as the men began bragging how they had taken down a group of 12 burly Aslaiks just the four of them. Pery received a big chunk of the credit, which he refused to own up to, instead turning their attention to the bravery of the other 3. The entire family *ooed* and *awwed* over the valuables they had raided from the demons; silk, jewels, weaponry, and magical items that weren't uncommon for the area. Out of all the items the four brought back, Aurora noticed that her partner hadn't taken credence over any of them for his work. He sat their quietly amidst the glory the other three were given of their family. An odd feeling began to grip Aurora about her companion; that he was holding back something or not letting on to the entire story. She wanted so desperately to ask what truly happened out there, but before she could raise the nerve, they were all piling out of the house onto the streets.

The sounds of celebration rang through the crowd as people danced their way down to the central streets. Wild colours and gaudy decorations flooded their senses. Aurora understood then why the merchants called their costumes *skins*, for each family was dressed in some form of wild beast. She glanced again at the attire in which her patron family was cloaked and felt stupid for not realizing sooner. The women wore a muted tan shawl of fur pinned together with bones, while the men, including Pery to Aurora's utter amusement, wore brighter and cruder versions from the women. All wore the crown of antlers she had seen previously.

Aurora had no time to gape over her brilliant realization, for they were being dragged down hill to the centre of the celebration. The closer they got, the more riled their neighbours became. Nerves began to ware on Aurora at the thought of being separated from the only people she knew in the town. A hand took hold of Aurora's as the attempted lion's roar of a family next to them vibrated through the energetic crowd. She glanced to her left and noticed Tori looked nearly as nervous as she.

"It's my first celebration too..." The girl whispered loudly. Aurora could feel the goosebumps raise on her arms and thought that Tori probably felt the same way. "... So who do you plan on courting?" The girl stuttered out quietly.

A rock fell in Aurora's gullet. "-What?"

Tori glanced to Aurora's stunned face, mumbling that they should stay away from the mice or any other rodents because it would make a poor match. Aurora gave a blank stare.

"You are a woman now aren't you?" The girl asked nervously as Aurora nodded dumbly, the same blank expression still plastered on her face. "That's what the costumes are for... to court your mate for a year and a day. If you get with child, then the costume will change to the mother's skins... but you don't have to finish the courtship!" Tori exclaimed hastily, seeing the green hue rise on the older girls face. "It *is* fun to flirt though." She finished with a shy smile.

"H-how old are you?!" Aurora stumbled out.

"Twelve, why?"

Aurora's mouth was flopping open like a fish. She snapped her wide-eyed gaze to Pery who in turn, had his attention focused on Kasha's ramblings, deliberately avoiding her piercing accusatory gaze.

The bastard knew... Jerk.

Everyone arrived at the square in a bustle of laughter and

tribal beats. Groups of girls traipsed around clutching onto goblets of dark spirits and skewers of meat, giggling their little fool heads off. The fire in the centre of the square rose three stories high, blazing brightly against the clear night sky. Heat from the blaze gave comfort to Aurora's reeling thoughts as she gently swayed in time with the rhythm. She always liked school dances but hated the censure of her peers. She relaxed a bit more. No one knew who she was here, no one cared if she looked like a big boob from her inferior dance moves, and if they did care, why should she? It's not like she would ever come back, as sure as she was of returning home after claiming finishing this odd journey of theirs. Why not let go?

The merchants group got bigger and wilder as the night pressed on, Tori introduced her to some friends, while Kasha ignored her completely to Aurora's relief. A knot formed in Aurora's stomach as Pery left to talk to a group of girls bedecked in hundreds of mice pelts. Wanting the feeling to alleviate, she grabbed the first glass of spirit that had passed her way. It was sweet yet tangy, with a hint of smoked cedar laced within it's splendour. It was wonderfully sinful, and hit her like a ton of bricks.

Flash backs of partying with her friends flew through her mind as the world grew brilliantly fuzzy and tipsy turvy.

"Shashi, what the Juda have you gotten into?!" Kasha guffawed regally as Aurora tried her damnedest not to run into the girl. "Have a seat, girl, and get some food in your gullet..." She instructed as she led Aurora to a side bench, shoving food in her ever-tilting sights. Kasha clucked over her like a mother hen as she forced Aurora to eat the dry as sin herb loaf, chunk by little chunk. A gruff hen, but still a hen none the less.

"Listen, Shashi, make sure to go back to Anni's by the blue flame alright? Promise me now, aye?"

Aurora nodded her head like a bauble as she muttered some expletives to herself. Kasha grunted and left for greener pastures, or rather, hotter company and Aurora grabbed another drink.

The night grew wilder as blatant make-out sessions ensued around the fire. Dancing became provocative and Aurora's eyes scanned the crowd of beasts for her friend; she had enough and simply wanted to pass out. Steeling herself in her drunken state, she dove back into the frey to ask one of the deer how to get back. Her gaze instead found Pery as he devoured Kasha's lips with his own.

Aurora's chest ached at the sight, wanting nothing more to go hide in a dark corner and cry her heart out. Abruptly turning away from the gut wrenching scene she ran into one of the men from the deer clan, who pointed the way back to Anni's. Nearly running from the spectacle, she dodged the drunken dancers and slowly began her ascension up along the rows and rows of elegantly styled homes. Glancing back over her shoulder, she noticed the flames had died down to an eerie blue and finally understood what Kasha was saying. They really did become animals in the light of those azure flames.

A hand snaked out from the shadows and snaked around her waist in a vice-like grip as someone pulled her into the surrounding darkness. A group of burly giants swarmed her; jeering and laughing darkly as they made quick work of her costume. Their breaths smelled of spirits and they way they laughed made Aurora realize she might not make out the night alive. Desperately she tried to escape the rough hands that fondled her and bit the hand that covered her mouth. The coppery taste of blood filled her mouth as she inhaled deeply to scream. A fist met with her jaw and she fell to the ground limp, the wind knocked right out of her and her world quickly going black. The last thought that crossed her mind was that she didn't want to die yet... refused to die... and that she would haunt the skuts who took her friends away if she did.

Chapter
Sixteen

The raging party unnerved Usellia as he slunk around in the bordering shadows. He watched the stupid boy slobber over the pretty deer as his Heiress gazed on in horror and left. Stupid, stupid friend; blind to all but his own stupid fascination with mistakes. He paid no heed to his companion's feelings, probably didn't even know she harboured any towards him. Dumbass...

Usellia kept to the shadows as he went after Aurora, the noise from the celebration blocking out any thought of concentration. When he rounded the corner, there was no sign of his quarry in sight. Panic flooded Usellia as he frantically searched all along the corner block, his heart dropping to his toes when he noticed the drops of blood in the dirt.

He followed the signs of struggle and the footprints that led back up the hill northwest of the main centre block. They were dragging something behind them as the path led to an old abandoned hall. The grounds were deserted and silent, except for the yipping of local wild dogs and the call of the night life. Usellia's blood began to run cold at the prospect of finding Aurora dead, or worse yet, broken in mind and spirit. What would these monsters do with her? Did he really want to find out?

No matter what state his Heiress was in, he would aide her willingly or not.

The shadows cast by the moon's plump belly cascaded around the stillness of the hall. Hiding in plain sight would be difficult for

Usellia if he was to find her before death did. A faint muttering of profanities and sharp orders crawled through the nearly empty hall, telling Usellia that they were in the room beyond. He slunk forward, taking the utmost care to not be heard and peered into the room.

It was completely trashed.

The once elegantly painted walls were stained with old blood and weapon marks marred the treasured artwork. The furniture and statues lay piled roughly in the far corner in front of a shallow arch that led out to the court room in days past. Windows were broken and barred from the inside. It was their lair, and if Usellia was ever caught, he would be slaughtered on the spot no questions asked.

There was four of them, all monstrously tall and thick like a century old tree. Their faces were hidden with masks and feathers as they hauled a sack into the corner opposite the arch, dropping it like a 50 lb sack of potatoes. A pained grunt escaped the bag as it landed with an audible thud upon the dust laden stone floor. Usellia held his panic secured behind that sound; Aurora was definitely alive, but just for how long? Should he go fetch the boy and his deer friends and leave her to succumb to the whim of these barbarians? Within an instant he knew that he couldn't leave her now. He was all she had.

"Dar, stop trying to fondle the girl and go keep watch!" The biggest of the brutes said in a heated whisper. The man grabbed the smaller man who was trying to get Aurora out of the sack and flung him effortlessly across the room towards Usellia. The pig stumbled to his feet and mumbled under his breath as he slowly trampled out of the room, unknowingly passing a very still Usellia as he went.

"Tok, Meeka, go get some food from the feast and some gear for the ride... we're leaving at first light." The brutes nodded and followed the pigs path out the room, once again bypassing Usellia's presence. In the darkness of the hall, the lamp the man coaxed to life nearly burned through Usellia's retinas. When the spots cleared his vision, Usellia's throat nearly clamped shut in panic as the man's growing attentiveness towards his Heiress' nearly naked form.

Boss-man towered evasively over Aurora's still form; not a single movement of muscle and an intensely powerfully hungry looked were etched int his face as he slowly scanned her flesh. With the speed of a cat, the barbarian strode over to Aurora and began to rip the sack from her, rough enough to leave Aurora gasping with pain from her unconsciousness.

"You're damn lucky my employer does not wish to see you harmed, young one." The man muttered hungrily into the stillness of night. "If I had it my way, you would no longer be breathing as I took you." Aurora herd the underlying threat and tried squirming away in a whimpering terror. Usellia was just about to leap into action when the man quickly stood and began tying her up with a string of bloodstained rope. Usellia could see the gag go across his Heiress' mouth and blanched at the blood upon her face. If he had gotten to her sooner, maybe none of this would have transpired. But maybe's never did cure the consequences of actions and never were any good for the there and now.

Boss-man carefully sat Aurora up and cockily strolled out of the room. Usellia's luck held fast as he swiftly crept to Aurora's limp body. With a deftness of years of knot-work he untied the ropes and undid the gag, slamming his hand to her mouth as she was about to scream.

"-Heiress, it be me." He whispered almost soundlessly as he tried to work her joints gently back into a mobile state. "You must flee and seek out the boy. I will make sure they don't follow." Aurora nodded silently and tried to rise, stumbling to the ground multiple times in her effort to run. Usellia rushed to her aid and helped her through a small gap in the wall beside the clutter of pews and statues, barely big enough for the two of them to squeeze through, but thankfully no one else.

"I'm going north." She slurred quietly at a wide eyed Usellia. "If I don't find Pery right soon, I will go without him. Tell him and meet me at the abandoned cottage." Usellia nodded agreement, trying to wipe the worry from his gut as he shooed her away. Even though he had no idea what she was talking about, he would relay the message if it meant his life. He watched her sink into the darkness as if she were a part of it and glanced towards the square. The adrenaline was waning and the roar of a furious leader noticing his quarry was missing was the only thing that got him to stay. She would not become the devil's play thing if he had anything to do about it.

◄Aurora►

Aurora heard the angry bellow of her captor as she raced towards her friend. Fear and a startling sense of clarity carried her through the waning crowd. No one spared a second glance at the girl in the shadows with a tossed demeanour. As she raced up the hill, bright eyed and ready to kill, she recognized a familiar voice muffled behind a caved in shed.

A small figure stood guard, cowering from all the noise and looting fiends. At the sight of Aurora, her face became alight with recognition, but was immediately squelched back into a panic.

"Aury, she's there- in there- get her out- get HER OUT!"

"Who's in-"

"Sansa! It's Sansa!" The girl cried, terrified over the youngest of her 5 sisters. "She came to sneak some food and there was a riot! So many people...Help her Aury, oh please help her!" Tears streamed down the face Aurora just then realized as Tori's. Without hesitation, Aurora delved into the battered shell of the building, throwing peices to the side as she slowly uncovered the battered body of the child beneith the ruins. Panic flooded her as the childs eyes remained firmly closed while Tori bellowed the girl's name in their ears.

Aurora had to repress the urge to curl up in the street and weep as she meticulously checked for breaks and bleeding. Sansa was whole and breathing, but the small cut and bruise on the side of her head might mean permanent damage. A loud creaking groan gave them enough warning to snatch the unconcious girl up before the building came crashing down over their heads. A whimper escaped from the darkness that surrounded them and Aurora was shocked to realize it came from her.

"Here, Aury, bring her through here!" Tori stated shakely as she ducked through an arched opening to some sort of stone temple. Litter scattered the ground from the celebration along side drunken bodies that were dosed with the love brew one too many times. Out of the stillness of the night rang an angry yelling from a not too happy boss-man. Aurora grimaced at the thought of getting caught again and what had happened to Usellia... and Pery.

The drunks mumbled and stirred in their sleeps as the two crept passed them, making their way to what must have been the infirmary. It was riddled with broken and bloody souls that had made the mistake of fighting while under the influence of stupidity. Everything was eerily shadowed by the dim light from wall scones almost burnt out of fuel. Gently, Aurora lowered Sansa onto a long bench along the far wall, Tori flitted about, not knowing quite what she should do.

"Get water, clean cloth and a blanket." Aurora said calmly, hiding the fear and rage securely behind a serene facade. Tori bolted to do her bidding as Aurora tried to rouse the still girl once more. Why anyone in their right minds would have such a celebration every single year was beyond intelligence; beyond common sense, hell beyond any kind of thought once or ever. These people should be ashamed of themselves for letting such a thing get so out of hand... unless this wasn't out of hand at all.

The stupidity of horny teenagers knows no bounds... And to think, she was still technically considered one of them.

Tory came racing back with arm-fulls of supplies and took a quick step back at the sight of Aurora's completely peeved face.

"I-I-It took some looking.." She stuttered unexpectedly. She didn't think she took *that* long. Aurora immediately masked her emotions and slapped on a look of makeshift relief as she arranged the blanket tightly around the still form. Aurora worked quickly with the cold water as she cleaned up the dried blood with numb fingers. She could see her breath, yet felt nothing but a rushing heat course through her body. A flash of warning seeped into Aurora's thoughts as she washed the last of the blood from Sansa's hairline.

"Can you keep watch Tori? There's people out there that are after me..." Tori's eyes came into focus, as if seeing Aurora for the first time, absorbing the state their saviour was in; dress torn askew with her own blood and bruises marring her skin. As Tori nodded her acknowledgement, she began to wonder exactly what god their people had angered to result in such a night.

As each moment flitted by, Aurora slowly ceased the fidgeting and simply stared into the sleeping face of the child in front of her. She was just a baby, maybe seven years old and so full of innocence. Uncorrupted by the violent and evil that marred this world so fully. She should have no worries in this life besides which flowers to pick for her mother.

"I wish I were like you Sansa..." Aurora whispered fervently, running cold hands along the child to keep her warm. "You have such potential and spark. I find myself shaken by the mere pretense of you here like this." The eerie stillness of the infirmary disturbed her, making every hair stand up on end. Silence cut through the dark and Aurora suddenly found herself staring into the clear eyes of a wise and knowing 6 year old. Aurora bolted to her feet in surprise and nearly tripped over herself as she mumbled happy nothings to the child. Sansa giggled roughly to herself over her caretaker's silliness and sprang to life, giving Aurora a much deserved embrace.

"are you gonna save us all from the darkness?" Sansa whispered shyly in Aurora's ear, face gaunt and haunted by the knowledge no child should have to worry over. Aurora glanced at the girl in puzzlement, unable to form words from her moving lips. "Mama has seen evil... real evil and she said that a hero will come save us. Are you a hero?" With eyes shining with hope and trust, Aurora feared to say anything and break that spell of innocence. She couldn't swallow away the lump in her throat. Was she a hero? Could she really save these people... govern them when it came down to it? Sansa gave a knowing smile and giggled her innocent laughs.

Tori burst into the infirmary, white as a ghost as a bunch of men made their way loudly through the rabble. The girl's face momentarily lit up at the recognition of her sisters consciousness, but didn't skip a beat as she ran close enough to not be overheard.

"There are men that say they're after a girl that escaped them." She gasped between breaths as the ruckus gradually grew louder. "Go, Aury- it's you they're after! Go Hide-RUN!"

The sound of the men boomed through the infirmary, stirring the drunken and injured from their healing slumbers. Every second felt like one too many as Aurora bolted through a crumbling archway into an outer garden that faced the open east horizon. All she could hear was her own frantic footsteps and heavy breathing. She thought that she heard Pery's angry bellow as the deep booming voice of the gang's boss-man crawled to Aurora's ears in the shape of a formidably dark laugh. Dawn was breaking over the horizon in all it's hopeful glory, giving way to the darkness and terror of that night. In the morning glow she would push forward into the unknown, and hope to God her two friends would find her alive and in one piece in the end.

Chapter
Seventeen

Pery caught Aurora's pained expression before the mass swarm of people swallowed her from sight. How stupid he was to flirt with temptation while his pride and jewel was drowning in the unexplored and completely new experiences of an outsider. She did not know how to defend herself, did not know that each move upon another signifies simplistic procreation of a bloodline, that would be absolutely barbaric and savage in her time and place. A child is raised by the mother's family here, the father means little to these villagers until a union is formed. Often times the husband is not the father of the children before, but blood-of-her-blood makes them his when the time ripens.

Kasha's arms clasped possessively to Peregrith's hips as she ground herself into him suggestively. Pery knew what Kasha sought and knew Aurora wouldn't understand the lightness of parentage, knew her innocence would not allow for there to be anything less than what he was so close to ruining between them. And there was something, by God there definitely was something there that Pery refused to ignore. And he wouldn't ignore it, so long as she didn't.

Pery took Kasha's face between his numb hands and kissed her painfully on the lips, a gaze in his eyes saying that he has made his choice. Kasha tensed and caught her breath at the unexpected pause, but understood why he was saying no. Men's heads can be fickle and too judgemental, but the heart knows what the head won't admit. Halla knows hers does. Kasha watched her heart rush into the frey of flaying bodies and shrivelled a little inside as the celebrations reached it's zenith. She wouldn't be part of the celebration this year and it stung to be so rejected in such a public fashion. Ignoring the increase in tempo and wildness, she slunk away from the hoard of bodies to join her sisters in blissful slumber.

Pery rushed through the seething crowd, trying to catch up to his companion, but to no avail. She was swallowed whole by the shadows faster than a person could blink and out of sight too quickly to discern in what direction she had taken. Panic began to flood his veins at the thought of her alone. Not everyone was rightly honourable when a lass tells him 'no'.

Darkness was no match for him as he used his blood talents to source her out. It was an old trick his family had once used to find a lost child or spouse. His focus became clouded as he searched for the trail of life force that wisped around each and every soul in Avalonia. Even with all the feral civilians weaving into his line of sight, he picked out Aurora's trail almost instantly. Racing after it like a hound on a scent, he hadn't noticed the three incredibly bulky men that stood in the wake of the crumbling building before him.

"Look at this here wee lad!" One of the brutes bellowed to his comrade as he stood there solidly, arms crossed and a mischievous grin on his ugly face. The man's broad edged sword hung loosely at his belt, awaiting action. Pery eyed him warily, his vision slowly going back to normal. Just at the last second, Pery recognized another life force trail he recognized. He had to think up something quick if he was to give Usellia time to help Aurora.

"Oi mate, what bring ye in dese 'ere parts?" Another of the thugs crooned darkly. Pery stood up tall and looked the three of them dead in the eye.

"I wanna join ye's b'ys." He announced unwavering. The three brutes looked on, dumbstruck, scanning this arrogant boy's bulk, or lack there of, and trying desperately not to laugh.

"-Bu' ye be puny boy!" The biggest of the three exclaimed

roughly, a look of disbelief firmly set in his stance. "If ye were mayhap twenty years elder and actually had meat on yer bones, mayhap lad- but ye be far too wee for this line o' craft ye be."

Oh if they only knew...

"-I be naught bad, whiff me blade!" Pery exclaimed with as much force as a chicken in face with a hawk "I'll show yeh!"

Pery released his hidden blade with the speed of a lightening strike and struck down a half leaning pillar in the same fluid motion. The men stood, slack jawed at the splendiferous speed this seemingly simple country boy exhibited.

"Seems to me, Gentlemen..." A low voice snaked its way up Pery's wary spine, "There is more to our lad that meets the eye..." A shutter ran through him as he forced himself to meet the man's gaze. He knew that voice, and dreaded the confirmation his glance granted him.

There, leaning in the shadows behind his men, stood Dalson, the leader of the Dark Sisters; feared by all who could still recount the grizzly tales of rage and murder. His skill and knowledge ran back nearly as far as his own, back to the Northern Wars some hundred years previous. If he didn't take care, Pery would be found belly up in the gutters this night.

"Do you seek serenity by our hands tonight lad? Is that why you show us such a blade?!" The man taunted, half teasing but in all deadly seriousness.

"-He's looking to join up, Boss." The smallest of the brutes said weakly.

Even his men are afeared around him... Pery thought glumbly to himself. *What a deadly dance this will be...*

"... No." The bohemuth proclaimed darkly. The air grew

heavy with anticipation of their boss' final ruling words. "I know why you've come, Peregrith, and you will not have her."

Within the blink of an eye, Pery lunged at the three easiest targets and knocked them to the ground with such grace and skill, it really did look as if he were dancing. Being too slow to react, they were down within three short breaths, which left Dalson leaning against a barricaded shop door looking on with approval at his magnificent opponent. An arrogant smirk emerged from his lips, head shaking with utter delight. It was sheer luck that he would run into his old-boyhood rival before Isietha got her claws into him. Though the boy didn't know it yet, he was in for a world of hurt once the witch reclaimed what was owed to her.

And Pery did know this. The stories and the legends of Dalson; the Fist, surpassed everyone's waking imaginations. It was said that he was the chief ruler of a large clan just north of the border before he joined ranks with the devil. Massive bloody slaughters flooded his lands and every other land his arrow chose. He was the harbenger of death and suffering, before the witches stripped him of his immortalizing powers; tossing him into the pits of a mountainous dungeon to rot. Obviously they hadn't locked it tight enough.

A glimmer of metal shimmered above Pery's brow as a swift sting marked his face. Pery was shocked to see a trail of blood travel along the side of his face, the pain not registering in the rush of adrenaline. *Enough play.* Pery thought to himself as a dark smile marred the boys lips. Within a beat of their hearts, Pery was gone from their senses. Not a trace lingered behind as the Boss glared wide eyed and furious at the empty space before them.

◆———————————◆

Pery's cheek stung with a throbbing rhythmic pain, dripping with his life blood and disappearing amidst his sweat stained clothing. If he wasn't careful, the poison that Dalson used would leave Pery dead along the gutters somewhere. Already the cut on his cheek began to fester and itch painfully. After two hundred and thirty years on this wide earth, you'd think a boy would learn from such a cocky mistake. It was many moons since Pery had come across a skilled hunter such as himself, most having been destroyed or banished from the isle during the reigning of Emilia's Blood. He retreated into the safety of shadows and the loud rumble of the crowds outcry below.

He silently dived into the heal-hall that housed the injured or too incapacitated to participate in the festivities turned flash-mob. All the poor souls of this hormone filled night lay still with an odd groan or the sound of vomiting thrown into the stench of blood and booze. Grabbing a small vial of 'heal-all', he moved to the nearest basin, washing the grime from his wound and applied the slimy gunk directly to the cut that was now a viciously widening gouge. The stinging intensified until he was all but outwardly yelling from the pain; teeth cutting into the flesh of his knuckles as he bit down upon his fist. The sound of approaching footsteps snapped him from his agony as he instinctively hid behind one of the upturned tables, hoping the Hunter and his gang hadn't followed him.

Silently he listened to two slight figures rush into the dim grungy room, pointedly rushing to the farthest corner from the exit and setting something down upon a half broken bench. The two muted voices exchanged terrified whispers before the smaller of the two rushed off for some unknown reason. The little light there was shone upon what Pery could now depict as a child, not more than five or six summers. The child lay deathly still, pale except for the obvious veil of blood soaking the child's hair. The figure kneeling before the child seemed familiar, but for the shadows cloaking their figure.

"-I wish I were like you Sansa..." a rough voice whispered through the hall. Perys head turned towards the source, recognition slowly finding him. His heart thudded heavily in his chest as he slowly peered over the barrier. There, sitting delicately beside the body of the child was the silhouette of a battered, bloody and bruised Princess. Pery nearly jumped out of his skin as the realization sunk in, but the anguish that formed around her cracked croaking voice halted his advances. Immediately his attention focused on the child. What was Sansa doing out on a night like this?

The sight of his companion in such a dishevelled, ground-out condition put pangs of regret through his gullet as he strained to hear what she had to say to the unconscious child. Words of self doubt and fear laced her thick voice as she confessed all that clouded her mind. Pery heard his name mentioned as a tear ran down her dirty bruised cheek. It dawned on him that it was his fault she ran into danger; her marred skin was crafted from his own egotistical stupidity. A stabbing sensation ran through his guts and he suddenly felt the age he really was.

A gasp of joy filtered through the packed hall as the innocent gaze of a very sweet girl brightened the room. Pery was about to stand and greet them when Tori burst into the hall looking as frightened as the deer her family represented. Within a moment, the sound of four deep and dangerous voices cut through the girls' frantic whispering. Another blink of an eye and Aurora was fleeing out a back entrance, Tori trying to act as innocent as possible as the Dark Sisters entered into the thick atmosphere if illness perspiring throughout the room. Pery glanced at Tori who tended her little sister while trying to play it as cool as possible.

"Where is the woman?!" One of the men boomed impatiently, producing a wave of grunts and complaints from surrounding patients.

"Who?" Tori answered in the most child-like innocent expression possible. The man growled as he stepped so close to her, she almost toppled over from the man's gravity. A small squeak escaped the girl as a massive hand lifted her off the ground effortlessly from her tanned collar. A sneer of superiority washed across the man's dirty, age honed face as he held it close to the child's.

"Don't make me ask again wench. You don't want to know what we do to dumb females, even one so young as you." Tori's face remained blank at the implication, but Pery's blood ran hot with fire. He promised himself a million times not to take another human life, but these monsters deserved no such humanity.

⋘Tori⋙

I don't know if I was knocked unconcious or if I had instinctively closed my eyes to the sudden movement from the shadows. All I knew was that suddenly there was darkness and the sounds of animals being sent to slaughter. I recall being curled up in a pool of blood that was not my own, and hearing the voices of creatures drowning in their own blood.

It took me an eternity to work up the courage to go to Sansa, and without knowing quite how I achieved it, I was huddled close with my baby sister in my grasp, unknowingly watching Death at his most finest form. Before I realized what I was seeing, the three men and their leader were on the blood soaked floor, ravaged by a creature cloaked in shadow with eyes glowing red.

"-Hero..." Sansa whispered in reverie at the splendor of such efficiency for Death. All that came to my mind as the man towered over the still corpses, blood dripping from the tip of his nimble daggar, was 'Demon'.

⋘Peregrith⋙

Peregrith could feel his ancestral blood beginning to heighten his awareness, making time shift ever so elegantly and giving an amount of focus so strong, humans would crumble under the attempt. He could hear the throbbing veins of the men standing before him coursing with the dark blood of the monsters they have become. He smelled the lust off the man that held his young friend. Each breath was longer and deeper, to better root his senses into what he was about to do. No guilt, no hesitation, only the knowledge of what needed to be done. He had to be quick if he wanted to take Dalson down.

With a movement as natural as breathing, he cloaked himself in shadow and with one graceful flick of his hand, decapitated the head of the man that held Tori. In the same breath, he silenced the other two before a word could be uttered by making an insanely precise incision along their larynx without nicking any major arteries. Frantically the two raced for the exit, stumbling over the head of their fallen comrade in their haste. The shadows swallowed Peregrith greedily as he vanished from their senses, only to appear in front of them in the breath of a heart beat.

Peregrith could smell the reek of fear from the two as he stared up into terrified gazes, glazing over in fear and panic, streams of blood dripping down their sweaty muscular necks. He wanted to toy with them, to listen to the little voices in his head to prolong their fear and do to them all that they had done to others. However quiet the voice of reason was to his ears, they still gripped him painfully at the knowledge of another looking on joyously at his game. With one more fluid move, he stepped between the two and cut them both vertically in twain.

The sounds of gushing blood and the faint mirth of an evil soul echoed within the hall. Peregrith vaguely recalled the people healing themselves in the building, the children he was bound to for protection. They were all silent, all huddled in the far corner out of range and mind. Dalson spoke no words but continued to laugh quietly upon life's own joke. Sweat began to perspire on Peregrith's shaded form as he glared at his last foe.

'It has come to this.' Dalson thought twistedly as he stared at his bygone men at Peregrith's feet. A look of bloodlust crossed Dalson's gaze as he drew his weapon ever so slowly from it's sheath, a crazed smirk on his war scarred face.

The raging shadows danced around Peregrith like smoke, clinging to his form as he slunk towards his vellicating opponent. To Peregrith's bitter surprise, Dalson began to be enveloped in the same dark mist that protected Peregrith so efficiently and fought with matching speed and vigor as himself. Bright red sparks of metal hitting metal showered over the silent battle, power sizzling as the blades clashed with the speed unintelligible to the human eye. The only things that could be distinguished in the battle between two torn heroes was the sounds those swords blade upon one another, like two wolves howling their thirst for blood.

Dalson halted their deadly dance and glared down at Peregrith with the same red eyes. Peregrith caught his breath as he watched Dalson slide his blade gently over his own flesh, the same crazed smirk marring his now twisted features. A slow growl erupted from the beast and he lunged again for his foe. Peregrith side-stepped just in time to avoid a gut wound, but not in time to avoid the gash that ran along his arm, the same spot Dalson had cut himself. Pain shot up Peregrith's sword arm, but no sound was uttered as per the custom.

The beast lunged again and again, faster and faster they danced those deadly steps until at last with one final thrust, the battle was decided. Dalson's swords hunger for flesh was quenched, but by the parting of his own masters hide. With one exhausted thrust, the beasts fierce head was parted from his frantic body and rolled dramatically to the pile of flesh that was once his comrades. The silent battle was finished and one of the last demons of the old world snuffed out of existence.

As Peregrith stood there amidst four brutally slaughtered bodies, the children he swore to protect stared in shock at the red eyed demon that, for one painfully still moment, would vanish out of their senses and step forever out of their lives.

Chapter
Eighteen

As the morning rays lit up the devastation of the night before, Aurora retreated amidst what was left of the gloaming light. Birds stirred from their slumbers and what seemed terrifying in the shades of night became peaceful and harmlessly tame. Ignoring the pain in her side and the general stiffness that followed her movements, she snuck to the outskirts of the town towards the ramblings and giggles of a group of horny teens skinny-dipping in the nearby loch. Snickering to herself as she grabbed the nearest set of cloths and bolting as stealthily as her sore body would allow, she couldn't help but imagine the dumbfounded expression of the lad once he found himself completely bare to the silly girls. Donning the alias of a local farm hand, Aurora made her way down the road away from her night of hell, praying that Usellia reached Pery and that they both had an inkling as to where she was going.

It was a bright sunny morning with larks and robins dancing and singing their fool hearts out amidst the trees. Fields of straw lay peacefully upon her left as the local forest sat expectantly on her immediate right. Between every segregated field was a strip of thick bushes that originated from narrow man made ravines running perpendicular from the main road. Wildlife frolicked amidst the cover the belt provided, not paying any heed to the lowly human passing by. And there was no one for miles in either direction along that road, which gave her pause.

Wouldn't it be hilarious if I were going completely in the wrong direction?

"Oi!... Oi there!" Called a young voice from behind a clump of trees. Aurora turned abruptly, nearly collapsing onto her face fro the sharp pain in her side. A boy no older than Tori scrambled up to Aurora, all innocent-as-a-puppy-dog and everything until he caught sight of her sorry condition. His bouncing black curls swarmed his brooding face as he assessed the girl before him, whom dressed as a man did.

"Why on Earth would ye be in that!" He muttered, more to himself than her. Aurora shrugged and couldn't meet the boy's eyes for fear of being recognized. With her luck, there was a poster going around of her with a big '*WANTED*' sign beneath it.

"Hmm..." The boy looked her up and down again, face bent in deep thought.

"-I need to get North." Aurora muttered as clearly as her bruised face would permit.

The boy's expression softened with a surprising amount of understanding for one so young and patted Aurora's ravaged hands. "My Ma was in your position, her man nearly beat her to death and took her valuables. I begged her to leave off from him, but she wouldn't listen. Killed the babe in her belly from the beatin'. Is that why you're tryin' to look like a boy?"

Aurora's guard fell a bit at the lad's hardship. "Aye, a gang was trying to..." She cringed at the thought but couldn't form the words. The lad nodded an innocents' understanding and tried to coo away the memory.

"Don't ye fear Miss. I have a hole out in the trees that you'll be safe in. No magic can get to you and you can wash up and heal yerself..." Aurora gave a small smile to the boy as he began walking backwards up along the path. "It's up ahead a quarter league, behind a huge boulder in the woods- you'll see it from the road... and you may wanna try fer a little more effort into lookin' the part if ye wanna start actin' like a lad."

With one final wave, the boy faded from sight like an old memory caught in the relapse of time. A shiver ran along Aurora's spine as the recollection of a very real touch from a spirit awakened her own beliefs, beginning to make her question what was real in this world. Taking a deep breath of the gloriously unpolluted country air, she decided not to dwell on it yet and quickly find some semblance of shelter before she collapsed. Glancing at her figure, she could see what the boy meant by throwing more effort into her disguise, hell her lumpy bosoms practically screamed to the world '*LOOK AT ME AND MY SEXY GIRLY SELF!*'.

With cheeks ablaze and a stiff gate, Aurora rushed down the road until she caught sight of a cart sized boulder protruding from the forest bramble, ten or so yards from the forest line. Carefully, so as not to trip over the mass tumble of roots and holes hidden by piles of leaves and vines, she made her way to her sanctuary. Sunlight filtered through the branches with the wind, making it seems as though a giant were breathing across the forests raised arms, creating a melody only those of the forest would love. Finally reaching her destination, she caught sight of a very welcoming stream a couple paces away from the natural outcropping that would serve as her shelter for the next few days.

To her disbelief and pure bliss, she found a stash of fresh apples and a broken jar of salve deep into the recesses of the rock. She was really beginning to love the helpfulness of ghosts as she applied the deep green goop to her bruised and savaged skin. It was cool upon her flesh and nearly instantly began to numb the area it was applied to. Even if it did smell five times stronger than menthol and ghost peppers, she would take what she could get.

Deciding to bind her girly *ta-tas* before she fell asleep, she removed the filthy garments that she '*borrowed*' and sloshed the offending cloths around in the pool of water that was probably meant for drinking, and hung them up on a firm branch beside the stream.

Her greasy locks of hair twisted around her as she stared at her dagger, mind bending and steaming on if she should dare. *'Mayas well look the part.'* She thought glumly as she took up the dagger in one hand and her hair in the other. With one swift motion, the years of caring for such long, luscious locks was resorted to a tangling clump of hair at her feet. A deep groan escaped her lips at the sight of what was, now shifted to the vision before her, staring out from the pools reflection. A filthy, bruised, simple boy with a swiftly healing black eye stared into the still waters. It was perfect.

After munching three apples and sending her hair to the wind, Aurora stretched along the leaf strewn ground, the canopy of rock guarding over her sleepy form. How nice would it be if she could wake in a couple hours feeling refreshed, sun shining bright, and reach the northern cottage with no mishaps or otherworldly encounters.

"Not bloody likely." She whispered to herself before falling into a brutally queer dream about laughing horses dancing the nutcracker in big fluffy tutu's.

Usellia watched Pery leave the silent hall with a look of death in his eyes, staring out into an empty nothingness neither he or anyone else but Pery could see.

"Peregrith." Usellia called gently as he emerged from the shadows of a tumbled stable. A low primal growl came from Pery as he turned towards the motion, immediately recoiling in recognition of an ally. Usellia halted in his tracks at the sight of his friend whose eyes held a faint glimmer of red that did not vanish upon recognition. Pery shook his head and began rubbing the bloodlust from his temples. One thing he hated about taking form was the slow transition back from it. A lot of innocent blood could be spilled in between if one wasn't careful.

"Have you seen the Heiress?"

Pery shook his head and tried focusing on the buildings around them, his comrade breathing a sigh of relief as Pery's face shifted back to normal.

"I watched her leave the sanctuary before I..." Pery fell speechless at his actions. Anyone who would witness what he could become would be terrified and he didn't want to frighten or even anger his only ally on this quest.

"... I have seen what your kind can do, but I do not hold ones inherent blood against another." He stated softly to the open air. "Now, the Heiress said something about travelling to some northern cottage. Know anything of it?"

"-Aye, I know where it is." Pery mumbled as he began to make his way through the rubble towards Anni's home atop the hill with Usellia following close in the shadows. The streets were either littered with half-bloodied people trying to sleep it off, or half-naked lovers trying to do the same. Looking at it now, Pery was praying to the gods that Aurora was spared from the worst part of such a night, but by the look of those bruises on her not a half hour prior, he was doubting it.

Anni's house came into view and that of the granddaughter Kasha, whom sat outside of the cobb hut, staring at a passing ladybug as it scurried from one dead leaf to another. In her hands she clutched firm the bags Pery came to claim.

"Fair morrow to a hapless nigh." She bid to him as he joined her upon the ground. Picking a lone flower beside him and silently placing it in her hair, he watched with a clenched soul at the tears that dried upon her cheeks by the gentle wind.

"Pray do not call forth what you do not wish know."

Another tear escaped their confines as she curled up within

herself and wept noiselessly. "It's her isn't it, you're in love with her!" She whispered, broken.

"I am helping her to attain what needs to be... Matters not if I love her or even hate her, but we are bound to each others fate." A sob broke through Kasha's reverie at his words. But as moments interlocked, she began to feel the truth in those words and felt a bit at ease by it. Wordlessly she handed Pery the packs and went inside, quietly shutting the door behind her.

Pery stood briskly and began strolling to the Northern road, feeling a pair of steely eyes watch his departure. Usellia moved to join him, cloaked in a corded blanket tied around his bony frame. No one blinked an eye at the two strangers leaving town, but Pery was glad for the silence and the beautiful day that blossomed to life before them. A smile formed on his weary lips at the sound of a child's ghostly laughter caught in the wind. No matter the state his Heiress would be in when they saw her again, he knew that the courage that had been buried inside her for so long was released; that she too could be freed just as he had by the acceptance of friends.

Chapter
Nineteen

Dawn broke through the treeline, shining through Aurora's heavy lids and jostling her awake. A mere intended couple hours had turned into sixteen, the chilled air forming frigid around her bared skin. Her breath catches at the recollection of all that had happened what felt like a lifetime ago. But there was no more to be done other than keep pressing on, so, stretching her sore muscles into a semblance of mobility. A great many bruises and cuts marred her skin, but no tell tale signs of breaks had surfaced, so she counted herself lucky for that.

Briskly she washed away the sleep in her eyes and gazed in amazement at the reflection staring back at her, nearly forgetting the transformation she underwent the day prior. Good. At least she wouldn't be recognized if she kept her head down.

Filling her stomach as much as she dared, she set off down the road once more. The only sounds coming from the overzealous birds and the stream that wove in and out of sight. Geese made their way back south, honking to each other for company. The lack of companionship she was beginning to feel all too keenly. Never in a thousand years did she think she would miss those two, but they had grown to be a comfort over the last couple of months; a sense of security in an unknown world. And with that thought, insecurity began seeping into her thoughts once more, even as the tougher side of her locked away her fears. After all, if you wanted something done, one should best do it themselves. In this case it was survival.

'Just suck it up, Buttercup' She thought mutely to her over-anxious mind.

Hours stretched on and the fields soon became scrub-land, too rocky for much of anything to survive save the originating tufts of grass and sickly, spindly looking trees. Barely a sight to splendour, except for the possibility of buildings amidst a clump of thick trees in the distance. It took her another hour to make it close enough to discover the tiny village was home to the very monsters that sought her life so very often.

Aslaiks.

Though they weren't quite like those that she had ever come across. Though rough and still vastly ugly, they appeared to be somewhat cleaner and, dare she think it, almost polite upon inspection. The wary expressions of those going about their business spoke of a biased caution towards strangers, not surprising seeing that it was usually the other way around when they were about. Bypassing any unwanted conversation with a tamed monster, she pressed on, head hung low in hopes of squelching any attempts at unwanted chatter. With just odd looks of caution and wary glances, she managed to cross through the village without uttering a single word to anyone.

Swiftly the landscape moulded back into forest and farmland, the day growing colder as it went on. Various cottages dotted the horizon, all of which seemed to currently be in use. Exhaustion was beginning to set in with the gloaming light as all hope of finding the cottage began to fade from Aurora's mind. Just as she climbed the last hill to search for a suitable campsite for the night, the sight of an abandoned cottage amidst untended fields came into view.

Aurora stepped from the safety of the road and down the overgrown trail leading to the cold and lifeless stone cottage placed in the centre of a lush meadow. Three steps into the fray, and she tumbled, not so delicately, head over heals over two immobile lumps. Cursing under her breath, she groans her way to her hands and knees, immediately recognizing the all too familiar lumps on the ground. The sleepy forms of her two comrades emerged from the mist, blissful smiles lining their still faces. Confusion warred with annoyance at the sight of her two friends who looked like they had passed out after having a night of partying.

"Pery." Aurora grumbled, annoyance radiating from her in droves as she tried unsuccessfully to wake him, pondering slapping the jerk awake as she poked, shook and pinched any bare flesh available. He didn't stir. Wordlessly she tried the same with Usellia, a slight twinge of fear gripping her guts into a vice like grip she was becoming all too accustomed to. The swirl of mist and little lights Aurora had dismissed as fireflies intensified, beginning to dance a disembodied silent rhythm she could somehow feel in her bones. Grabbing one arm of each of her friends she tugged with all her strength towards the meagre shelter not 50 feet away amidst the mist.

The silent rhythm began to take form as corporeal figures of dancing lights added in their haunting melodies of voices long past. Aurora's desperation began to take it's toll as tears began to cloud her gaze. She could feel the spirits' spells beginning to work upon her as her thoughts began to fog, like the mist that threatened to engulf her into the abyss that was beyond closed eyes. With one last tug, the three of them tumbled over the threshold of sanctuary. Hurriedly she barred the door and shuttered the broken window in a near stupor, stumbling over her comrades while trying not to do a face-plant into the fire-pit as she tried to shed some light around their current predicament.

Glancing out what remained of the window, she gazed in awe at the tiny figures dancing amidst the meadow surrounding the cottage.

Fairies. As she lived and breathed, they were fairies... and they had almost gotten her.

With a sigh she took out the blankets and tucked them around the still bodies, hoping to stave off the growing chill. She prayed the spell would break come morning.

After cooking a glorious mass of oatcakes, she stoked the fire one last time before closing her weary eyes, thanking the Gods nothing worse had befallen any of them.

◆————————————◆

The morning came in cloudy and damp as Aurora opened her bleary eyes to the accusative glares and silent frowns. The spell was certainly broken as Pery and Usellia stared cautiously at the stranger curled up across from them.

"G-morning..." She grumbled with a croak as she stretched away the stiffness of an awkward fireside sleep. Recognition formed on their faces as their jaws dropped to the dirt.

"It's you!", "Heiress!" The two called out with a start, both nearly stumbling into the crackling fire. She smiled bleakly, still worn and frail from the last collective nights. Glancing at the fresh rabbit ready to be roasted, she readied the meal in silence, giving the boys time to recoup from their obvious shock.

"Those were fairies out there last night, weren't they?" Aurora stated calmly, more out of the need to fill the silence than recognition.

"Aye, Lass." Pery muttered, still slack-jawed from shock. "They keep the gates between worlds." Aurora swallowed hard at the memory of the night before; the familiar feeling before being pulled through the mists; before she arrived in a completely foreign world.

"... One can't avoid such a thing I'd suppose." She said to herself more than the others as she set the meat upon the now comfortable flames. The other two remained silent as the gristle began to sizzle amidst the flames. "Why couldn't they get into the house last night?"

Pery pointed towards a sprig of herb dangling above the doorway, old and dusty and unrecognizable to anyone but those that knew what it was for. Her mother used to hang rosemary above doorways to ward off sickness and dark spirits. Seemed the tradition wasn't too different there. Not surprising in a world filled with so much magic. Aurora's heart dropped a bit when Pery couldn't look her in the face. Whether by shame of the nights prior, or just not wanting to look at her ugly, now boyish features, it made little difference. What ever had snapped in Aurora to finally straighten her spine and grow the hell up, also made her want to close her heart to anything resembling love ever again.

Better to just rub out the bruises and forget about it, would probably be safer in the long run after it's all said and done. I'm too young for love anyways. Aurora shook herself mentally. *So no more... no more talk about love... Bet he doesn't even kiss well anyways...*

Chapter Twenty

Waking up to a barely lit fire, Pery's heart skipped a beat as eyes fell to a huddled mass of blankets lying wheezing beside them, sound asleep. Memories of the nights earlier flashed in front of his eyes.

Aurora gone.

The mounting fear.

The mist.

Oh Gods the mist! How did they escape it? To his left was Usellia, still sleeping as soundly as ever, while their supplies lay securely by the fire, seemingly still in one piece. Had they been saved by this stranger? What would he want in return? And where was his Princess?

Swallowing his deep fear and terror for a helpless lass, he snuck out the door into a world frozen by frost, instantly clearing his head of all things emotional. A rabbit nipped at frost covered greens outside it's burrow, not 20 feet away. The perfect meal for an early morning start.

The morning sun shone upon the earth, casting a luminous glow upon the reflective ice flakes, giving the world a soft dreamlike appearance while the morning birds did their duties. A fog of breath arose from Pery as he patiently stalked his prey, elegantly gliding close enough that he could almost step on it if he went any closer. With a flick of his wrist, a dagger flung through the air, piercing the now twitching rabbit to the bleeding earth. Swiftly dispatching it's life and saying a quick prayer of thanks for the easy meal. He never knew exactly what god was listening, if any at any given time, but thought it best not to tempt the powers that be by not acknowledging them.

Thoughts of Aurora's face at the festival kept streaming through his head as he cleaned the carcass. How foolish and selfish to put his own primal wants before the protection of the realm. One night of pleasure was not worth the future of his princess; his Aurora, whom had such hurt in those eyes, he wouldn't be surprised if she never spoke to him again. Though she would probably be safer hating him, since marriage would never be possible-

Wait what?

Since when did he ever want to give up his freedoms? A hard laugh escaped his lips as he shook his fool head. There was no future for the two of them. He couldn't even lie to himself about how much he cared for her. If only fate didn't play so thoroughly into their lives. He loathed the day they would part. But first, he would have to deal with the stranger that had saved him... then he would find his precious princess.

Pery quietly crept back into the cottage, taking care not to wake the lad as he slept like the dead beside the smothered embers. Smoothly he sat beside Usellia who was now wide awake and staring unbidden towards their guest, whom was beginning to stir. Pery held his breath, muscles tense at the possibility that friend might very well turn into foe. In the thick tension laden air, a familiar face looked out from the dirt smudges and day old bruises.

"G-morning..." Came an all too familiar voice from across the flames. Pery's heart skipped a beat as his princess gazed sleepy-eyed at the two of them. She had saved them... Had survived such royally deranged events and, through it all, had managed to save THEM.

By the Gods she was safe.

After the initial shock wore from the two, the need for proper rest and recuperation resulted in the three of them staying in the security of the cottage for five blissfully relaxing days. To Aurora's utter delight, Usellia showed her how to make a bruise balm out of some wild herbs growing among the meadow grass, resulting in Aurora being able to move without wincing and complaining under her breath with every step. The pelts from the seven giant rabbits the three of them trapped the first day had resulted into three pairs of gloriously warm mittens and fuzzy cowls that took the chill from the slowly increasingly cold nights. Mending, washing, sharpening and fixing all the things that needed it, the three of them worked tirelessly to prepare for their next leg of adventure up til the last night which they spent doing nothing more than relaxing by the fire with some beautiful, yet odd sounding melodies.

The seventh morning had come in bright and eager as they gathered their belongings and regretfully left the soothing comfort of the little cottage in the meadow. Making their way to the Northern Needle, a long and narrow strip of land towering above where two roaring oceans collide. Being only a mile in width and nearly 7o miles long, it would take them three sleepless days to cross and another five days to reach. From there, it would be simple for them to travel the highway along the coastline up to the Isle of Fire.

Hah, if only it were that easy.

They made good time during the daylight hours, each counting down the days til they reached The Needle in their own subtle ways. Pery getting gloomier with each passing sunset, Usellia whittling figurines each night by the fire, and Aurora making a chain of leaves and hanging them around the trees from sheer boredom. At night they would huddle close to the flames and would tell campfire stories to keep their thoughts away from the danger that always surrounded them; always keeping them on high alert.

Each morning left them aching and cold as the frost would paint the autumn landscape with a tinge of pure winter white. Pery sent a prayer up to whom ever was listening to halt any thoughts of it snowing before they cleared the Pass. He really hoped someone up there was listening.

Knowing that they were being hunted by the enemy's shadow hunters made Pery extra nervous as every night they stopped to make camp, came and went. If people thought aslaiks were bad, shadow hunters were so so much worse. Trained assassins, they were half-bred aslaik ninjas that were sent when the original baddies would fail. Thankfully they couldn't travel in sunlight, else Pery might actually be breaking a sweat. However, the danger was still there and made him increasingly on edge the closer they came to the eye of the Needle.

"Tell me again why we couldn't ride a horse or something this far?" Aurora whined, hauling her exhausted body behind the other two.

"... It's not like there was any to be had, Lass." Pery mumbled as he scanned the surrounding tree-line for the millionth time that day. "Our little peninsula is a poor area with few animals that could be spared for something as simple as walking." Aurora sighed loudly at the disapproval laced in Pery's voice. How was she supposed to guess these little quirks that so often showed up in this bazaar world they were in? And if this peninsula was considered small, she hoped with all hope that she could find a horse somewhere before her feet fell of... or a cow... hell even a fricken ostrich would be better than nothing. Actually an ostrich would be wildly awesome...

They pressed on through the night, covering a surprising amount of ground in the semi-darkness. The moon was nearly full as it guided the three with majestic glowing rays of light. If it weren't so cold and exhausting, they could have almost enjoyed the moonlit stroll.

In the small hours of the morning they reached a wide gap between two interconnected rows of mountains lined up like soldiers upon the coastline. The clear night sky was quickly becoming overcast and the convenience of the moon's light faded. Grabbing a few hours sleep appeared the wisest as opposed to getting lost in the gloaming light. With no fire and nothing but the sounds of the night life surrounding them, each quickly fell into an uneasy sleep in the pitch.

◆────────────────────➤

The morning light banished all unease of the darkness as the splendour of the area hit Aurora full force. Standing tall and proud, flanking both sides of the entrance to the pass stood two giant statues made of the same blue rock of the towering mountains around them. Clad in chain-mail and finely detailed armour, the medieval warriors stood tall at the foot of their charge. Their swords embedded into the earth before them, at rest beside their guarded path. Majestic as the wilds around them and as formidable as I'm sure the road must be.

They moved quickly onto the path that wound around the native rock, not coming across a single soul upon the road as hour after hour ate up the morning light. Stopping for short meals and light doze to ward off exhaustion, they walked as quickly as their weary bones allowed. Two agonizing days passed with this scheme while all of their instincts were yelling at them that they were being followed. Nerves remained on edge at the thought of being encircled with no way of escape save the rampant ocean's waves.

Noon came quickly on the third day as they stopped at a bottomless stagnant pool off the northern coastal shore. The warmth of the suns rays chased away the cold of the ocean breeze brushing across their flesh. Silence engulfed the three of them as they ate their cold oatcakes and dried meat. The sheer exhaustion was lost on no one as dark circles showed evident under all their eyes. Staring into the still waters of the pool, Pery wished for nothing more than to magically awaken at their destination, belly full and warmth encompassing all three of them. It ran through his head that it might have been easier to hail a ship to cross the waters, but the northern fishing islands still remembered his name, his face... what he'd done.

Snapping out of his revelries of past mistakes he noticed that in his mindful absence, he was staring at a pair of curious glowing eyes. Instinctively he flinched back and watched in shock as the eyes disappeared into the depths of the deep pool. A chill ran along his spine as to what the creature was. They were too far east for the water dragons, and the porpoises were too big to get into such a pool. Maybe it was a ghost, come to haunt him in a frighteningly dangerous form? The more he thought of them, the more he saw those ghostly eyes coming closer and closer to him until, to Pery's utter dismay, they rose from the water upon a sleek scaled head of a long serpent-like creature.

Both Aurora and Pery scurried back from the pools edge at the sight of such a gloriously dangerous looking serpent. Though as scary as it seemed, there was no identifiable air of danger or predatory need radiating from it. Almost as though it were a simple child, curious of a new pet it wants so desperately to bring home. The creatures head rose above the water, bobbing and weaving from side to side almost like a charmed cobra. It was the colour of the sea; a muted collection of greys, blues, and greens.

Nariel. Echoed through their minds, not as words but as a collection of feelings and emotions translated into languages of tongues.

"Nariel?" Aurora said back, stunned that she could understand it. Suddenly pictures of the serpent flashed through their minds at a blistering pace, of this young serpent interacting with others of the same kind, only vastly larger. Others of it finding various animals along the coastline and other saltwater pools; like the large lake they had travelled around, meeting with the unicorn mother that protected her home, and other places and animals Aurora couldn't recognize. An image of them shot through their minds with a curious inquisitive feeling swirling around it.

"I'm Aurora, and this is Pery." Aurora stated clearly, hoping that this creature would understand and hopefully wouldn't eat them. "I've been sent to help Avalonia... to stop Isietha."

The curious air around the serpent grew panicked and cold. Images of a tall figure cloaked in shadow and death passed through their minds along with a rapid succession of gory images of slaughtered creatures and poison, pointless death and pain. Anguish washed over them like a titanic tsunami of ocean waves that carried with it every serpents feelings and memories of pain and death. Aurora crumpled to the ground, staggering Pery to near unconsciousness, until tears began to rush down Aurora's face.

"-I will stop it." She gritted from the pain. "But I need to get stronger first."

The pain from generations of memories subsided slowly as Auroras mind began to clear.

"We need to get to the Isle of Fire."

◀Usellia▶

Usellia came upon his two friends talking with a serpent. A bloody serpent! And surprisingly not getting eaten in the process. It was a shame he couldn't marvel over it, but they needed to go. The hunters were almost upon them.

"Lad, Heiress... Dragon... we need to leave now."

The serpent darted it's gaze towards the interloper and growled. Usellia broke into a cold sweat but stood his ground.

"This is Usellia, he's helping us as well."

Nariel backed off a bit, tilting its large snake-like head and glancing back to Aurora as if in question as to why. Usellia ignored the jibe to his ego as he emphasized the need to flee once more. The serpent gazed to Aurora, as if talking to her without words. How delightfully bazaar...

Aurora turned to the others with a smile on her face, a flicker of hope in her gaze, "Nariel can take us." She stated with a huge grin on her face. Usellias jaw nearly fell of his face at the thought of it. What on earth did he miss while he was scouting anyways? Before any of them could second guess anything, Nariel began to morph into something bigger and a lot more deadly than Usellia ever wanted to ride, let alone look at. But the nagging realization that it was either trust in his heiress' instincts or keep running without them, left him taking a chance that they were being led straight to their deaths.

The sound of hoof-beats range through the ground as the urgency to go climbed to a whole new height. Glancing to the now fully transformed dragon, with spines and claws and everything scary, he couldn't help but laugh at the foolishness. But foolish or not, he climbed atop the spiny beast with the other two and hoped for the best. As he looked behind them and took in the swiftly disappearing sight of the nine cloaked hunters, a smile crossed his frozen lips as they escaped them yet again.

Cold ocean spray sprinkled their faces as Nariel glided unnervingly fast over the ocean waves. The three of them watched silently as the land slowly drifted further and further away, the cold ocean air making them second guess the rapidly made decision. Aurora prayed that the young dragon would actually bring them to the island, where ever it may be, and not directly to some other nasty thing that wanted their heads. At least if this did work, they would get to the isle in record time...

If they didn't freeze first.

End of Book One

Lightning Source UK Ltd.
Milton Keynes UK
UKHW020955090619
344088UK00005B/80/P